I0653634

The Fight For Silence

Roisin McCrink

Published in 2011 by New Generation Publishing

Copyright © Roisin McCrink 2011

First Edition

The author asserts the moral right under the Copyright, Designs and Patents Act 1988 to be identified as the author of this work.

All rights reserved. No part of this publication may be reproduced, stored in a retrieval system, or transmitted in any form or by any means, without the prior consent of the author, nor be otherwise circulated in any form of binding or cover other than that in which it is published and without a similar condition being imposed on the subsequent purchaser.

www.newgenerationpublishing.info

For my family and friends:
Thank you for always believing in me.

Chapter One

At seventeen I was suffering from the incessant rituals of torture that my parents had strictly followed. I had come to adapt to my surroundings and my circumstances, like the Darwinian Finch in the Galapagos Archipelago: my eyes focused on any sign of movement, as fear made them seek danger long before it found me; the hearing I had was excellent, due to the fact I had to prepare my body for pain the moment I heard the blade of the knife leaving its wooden case.

As sui generis, I was unique and one of a kind. My jaw was tight and cramped when I was asleep, a sign that stress never let me truly rest. The teeth in my mouth would grind in my sleep, and I would purse my lips as a result. I tried to hide any sign of weakness or pain when I was awake, which was a pathetic attempt in retrospect. Thus, I awoke from my sleep most nights to the blood-curdling screams that I would realize were my own. I didn't have any friends; I only had the wolves in the forest, who howled in reply to my screams. They could be heard viciously growling from the forest's edge when my torture sessions commenced, making me have more respect for wild wolves than humans.

Silence was my most loyal companion, apart from my shadow, and it gripped my hand as I endured the ferocious pain. The Silence shared my most inner fears, secrets and hopes, and when I escaped from the house on my eighteenth birthday, it promised to fight with me, and stay with me. Silence had its own language, and when Silence was allowed to speak it said more in a whisper than all the words spoken in a lifetime. The Silence talked to me. The full conversations it had with me allowed my mind to shed its boundaries and it spoke of how I was to be free. Then I realized my mind had opened up and I was free—or, as I realized, the term was psychotic.

I accepted my "psychosis" at first, realizing there was not much else to do about it. Then I began to love it. I was my own best friend, and I even had arguments with my inner mind; my inner mind being different from the 'normal' me.

It was the wolves that finally finished the process for me, and finally gave me the escape that I had been waiting for. I had awoken one night, and heard them sneering at the forest's edge. Instinctively, I had thought that my senses had lapsed and my parents were there to torture me while they had caught me off my guard. It turned out my parents weren't there, and the wolves were simply howling and making their low guttural growls at me.

I heard a thunder of paws on hard ground; the wolf's leaps muffled slightly by the moist grass. My skin tensed and tightened, as if there was space beneath my skin, like a vacuum, and my bones and tissue were numb and unreceptive. The huge black wolf leapt to my window, clinging to the ledge with his sprawled paws. He managed to hold on and hoisted himself through the window. I didn't fear him. In retrospect, I wondered why I hadn't been afraid of him in that instant, but I had faced worse horrors than the wolf before me.

The wolf's piercing blue eyes met with mine, and for a moment we locked contact, before blinking at the same moment. The wolf jumped to the floor and the hard pads of his paws crackled over the broken glass on the nearby floor from his forced entrance. He leapt forward, his body a foot above the floor as it glided towards me. The skin around his mouth drew back and he bared his teeth with a growl. Instinct pummelled ahead of reason and I did what came naturally to me in that instant: I snarled back. The wolf stopped short of me and stared at me, with a surprised and curious glint in his eyes. He blinked as if he had understood me. I blinked back, not realizing I had done so until I had missed the wolf's plunge for my wrist.

He had sunk his razor sharp teeth into my skin and scraped along my bone. I winced but I had felt worse. His eyes never broke with mine. As he opened his jaws, he licked my blood from his white teeth and blinked. I wouldn't say it was pain that I had felt, just a feeling of pin-pricks in my wrist that ran up to my shoulder. The wolf brushed his tail against my wrist as he turned back. The moon was shining through the window and as the wolf turned back to look at me for the last time, he tilted his head up, and howled to the moon. As he did so, I found that when he had stopped howling that I had been howling with him.

6

He blinked at me, and jumped out of the window, galloping back to the call of his pack.

The feeling that had encapsulated my right arm then began to spread through my body, and a powerful surge of anger and strength surged through me. I heard my parents' footsteps torture the floorboards as they moved; their creaking screams always anticipating mine. But the screams that were to be heard were not mine, they were my parents'. They entered the room, their shocked expressions falling on the blood, glass and paw prints of blood spotted on the stone floor, from me to the window. My father raised his fists towards me, as he towered over me in his usual fashion, and my mother wore her malevolent expression that I had so frequently been the receiver of. Then she reached for something from inside her dressing-gown, and retrieved a large bread knife. With snarling grins they began to descend on me. Suddenly, like a seismic tremor from within me, I felt power and strength overwhelm me from inside my chest.

"Bring it on! You two are so pathetic."

They laughed and I shook with fear as I tried to comprehend why on earth I had spoken. Then another surge of power and strength ran through me, and this time I acted on it. I leapt forward, punching my father in the face as I kicked the knife out of my mother's grasp. I grabbed the knife and threw it out of the window. The second I had thrown it I realized what a stupid idea that had been. I could have used it, but that didn't matter any more, I had to fight them properly now, not with their gadgets or torturing tools.

I had winded both of them with simultaneous kicks to their stomachs. They keeled over, and as they fell to the floor I broke both their noses with my knees. I was my mind's eye, watching it all happen, having hardly any control over my actions. Then I heard him talk to me. Rupert was talking to me.

Finish them off! Now is your chance to be free! Yes! Look at them now, writhing in their pathetic weak bodies! Come on Robert, you can do this! I'm with you now. We'll be together, I'm with you!

I felt the strength inside me burn like a fire, fuelling my hate for the foul creatures that lay before me. As they screamed and wailed, my mother spat words from her bloody mouth.

"Robert. Please don't hurt us!"

I reached out and grabbed their throats. Their screams were horrible to my ears, their shrill pitches searing through my mind.

"Shut up." I said. Their screams did not fail. I held their throats in my hands and tightened my grasp. Then their voices fell to a faint cry. "I'm fighting to never see you again! I'm fighting for the one good thing that's come to me these past years—I'm fighting for Silence." I said as I tightened my grip around their necks.

My ears found their heartbeats, and I listened as I heard their hearts slowly cease to beat. Their bulging faces relaxed as I let them free from my strong grasp. As they fell on their sides, I noticed their fingers were still poised in the position they had fixed themselves in when they were clawing at my wrists. I walked over to the window and smiled as I saw the black wolf, which I had called Rupert, stand at the forest edge, his head raised and howling to the moon. I had called the wolf Rupert because I knew that was the name of the second-me—the new me. I realized I was schizophrenic at that stage.

The wolf had given me some kind of animal strength that night, and as I sat by my parents' bodies, Rupert and I talked about everything. Days passed, and my wound healed, my mind was free, and yet I couldn't find the strength to leave the house. I waited for some sign from the woods. But no sign came. I looked continuously for Rupert the wolf, but I couldn't find him. I waited for a month, the stench of the rotting bodies beside me corroding my lungs more than the torturous deodorant had done. I had waited for the full moon, sleeping outside, just beyond my window. The nights were warm at my skin, even though there had been snow creeping over the surrounding peaks. Then I decided to leave. I was going to go into the woods.

"You have me now, Robert. You don't need to question things, accept them, live with them and embrace them!" Rupert constantly told me.

I had walked towards the forest's edge and then had begun to run towards the darkness. I started into the night; my sight in the darkness was enhanced since the bite. I ran for what had seemed like hours. My legs had galloped at high speed as I darted through the trees, but my heart beat remained regular and calm. I had felt more alive than I had ever done. I had Rupert with me, my new self, and as it had promised, the Silence was always to be found.

I had confessed to myself, or rather to Rupert, that I had been remarkably strong when I had killed those two, and that I had *loved* it. I had felt so proud of what I had achieved. Rupert and I forged a plan, as we sat amongst the trees on the mossy forest floor that we would fight for Silence always, as it had been the one companion that had helped me through it all. I had begun to worship the Silence then, lying carelessly in the heather that had engrossed the roots of the ancient trees, which proved to be rather comfortable sleeping areas. I worshipped the moon, and I often heard the gentle rhythm of the water as the stream trickled from the higher ground, which awakened my appreciation of sound, but not noise; after all, sound is only another form of Silence, noise on the other hand, is like crude graffiti on a timeless work of art.

I didn't know how they eventually found me, but the police cornered me as I was lurking in the shadows of the trees, their night-vision proving to be just as good as my own eyesight. This capture, in time, would turn out to be just what I had wanted.

Rupert and I had decided that it would be best if Rupert took hold of the situation, as he was stronger and better with words. I trusted him more than I trusted myself. I talked to him from the inside, like he had talked to me before, but the world only saw him, which I preferred, and which Rupert loved. He had everything that I lacked, so we decided he was the better man for the job.

Chapter Two

"No way, I'm not going to take his case," said Jim Price to his Supervisor.

"This is your job, Price. Lawyers train for years and don't get the opportunity you're getting now. Swallow your fear, or whatever you're feeling, and do the job you became a lawyer to do." Price's Supervisor bellowed from behind his desk. Jim Price swallowed the growing fear and spoke with a shaking voice.

"Sorry sir, I truly am grateful that you're giving me this opportunity."

"Here's his file. Take it, Price. I know you can do this, and I know in your heart you're dying to get at this creep. We both know that he is a creep, but he's been tortured, and that's why he is the way he is. Make the judge see that he's mentally unstable and you'll be making more money than you and your wife could ever have hoped for."

Price took the file from his Supervisor's hand, and surrendered to the curiosity that replaced the fear that was overwhelming him. He felt adrenaline rush through his body as he opened the file and saw Rupert's menacingly green eyes staring back at him. He smiled as he knew he would have no problem convincing the jury that this young man was a mentally unstable.

However, Jim Price found it a more challenging case than he had originally suspected. But, in the end he persuaded the judge to deem Robert Norton:

"Not guilty for the charge of first degree murder, but for Robert Norton to be treated for mental instability."

As I sat in my assigned seat, I could feel the hearts of the jury, the hearts of the other people in the courtroom and the judge's heart speed up as words left my lips.

"I want to stay in Scotland."

"Excuse me?" asked the Judge; her heart skipping a beat with every word I uttered.

"I want to stay in Scotland," I repeated my words a little louder.

"Robert, please, will you remain silent?" Price pleaded as he gave me an anxious look. My heart sped up and I could feel the anger swell as if it had been injected into my muscles.

"You remain silent, you cowardice fool," I said, standing up from my assigned seat.

"I would advise you to keep quiet, Mr. Norton. I would also advise you to remain seated," said the Judge from her elevated seat.

"Who do you think you are?" I asked as I stared at the judge, the words spilling from my lips before I had a chance to contain them; the anger growing steadily from within me. I could feel my muscles clench and unclench as I stared at the people in front of me. I could feel the strength in my muscles build, and I wanted to release my power on those who dared to order me.

"I am the Judge, and this is my Courtroom. If you want your freedom bestowed upon you this day, you had better keep your mouth closed."

"I believe it was Franklin. D. Roosevelt who said that 'Freedom cannot be bestowed; it must be achieved.' Any freedom that I have is the freedom I achieve for myself, not the freedom bestowed upon me by a pathetic excuse for authority."

In one fluid motion she held her hand up to security as they began to walk towards me; they stopped and awaited further signal.

"Why?" asked the Judge. Price's face was gleaming with sweat as he distanced himself slightly from me. I looked to my right and stared into his scared eyes. His pupils dilated as he looked into my fiery, yet calm eyes. I smiled from the corner of my mouth, and whispered to him. When I spoke the world around us withered away, and at that moment there was only Jim Price and me, whispering to each other—both of us transfixed by my threatening, yet luring manner.

"Are you scared?" I whispered to him.

"Yes," Price replied after a hesitation that seemed to have been caught in his throat.

"I can hear the blood pulsating through your veins—you're not scared enough. I'll have to change that," I said and my small smile widened, and then we returned to reality.

"Why?" the Judge repeated her words, this time with more conviction.

"What?" I replied, looking at her from under my dark eyebrows.

"Why at the last moment, when the Court has ruled in your favour, do you decide to distance yourself from freedom?"

"Perhaps the Court hasn't ruled in my favour," I replied, staring at her puzzled expression.

"Do you want to be sent to jail?" the Judge asked, her interest in me increasing.

"No."

"Then what would you prefer?"

"I would prefer," I began, as my smile widened to a grin. "I would prefer to silence you and every other imbecile who attempts to destroy the Silence that I have created for myself in Scotland — in *my* land. I know these lands, I know that I can't survive anywhere else than in Scotland and her shores."

"And how would you manage to 'silence' us 'imbeciles', as you call us?"

"Kill you," I answered.

A deafening silence filled the room as every gaze fell on me. I could feel it burn on the back of my head. Then, like a surge of water, the voices in the courtroom continued to crescendo as panic and fear became tangible in the air.

"Robert Norton, I find you in contempt of this Court. Take him away," the Judge screamed. Her final words reached a shrill pitch so as to be heard above the wailing of the distressed that surrounded us. I laughed as the police men ran towards me.

"My name's Rupert."

I felt my strength exert itself and I placed my hands on the desk and threw my legs over. I pushed off and I flew through the air, turning my body for an ultimate impact. My feet smashed against the jaws of the large men who tried to capture me. My fists met their bodies, and they were astonished as they had never met strength like mine before. As they lay on the floor, I grabbed their pulsating necks. My arms lifted them up from the floor and held them on their knees. Their fingers tried to prise mine from their necks, but they were unsuccessful. I looked at the screaming Judge and then at Jim Price. Their eyes were wide, and their lips were quivering, but their bodies were immobile; frozen in fear and distress. Tears ran over my fingers as the guards took their final gasps at air.

"I may be young, but I assure you, if you do not shut up I will silence every single person in this place." It took a few seconds for the roars and wails to reduce to mere sobs. "Stop sobbing," I said, directed at the women on the balcony behind me. I walked to the door of the Courtroom.

"Where are you going?" Price shouted from his seat. His voice was hoarse and weary after the sight he had just seen.

"Oh, I'm not going *anywhere*," I said calmly as I turned the key in the door to lock it. A rush of nervousness swept through my spectators. "Keep silent everyone." I walked up to the bar and sat behind it, looking at the tear stricken faces of the people in front of me. The Judge, to the left of me, remained facing forward as she was refusing to look at me.

"He's going to kill us—" a woman from the balcony said, but she was cut off by her neighbour clamping a hand over her mouth. She struggled free as she ran to the stairs that led her to the door at the far end of the courtroom. The mass of people tried to stop her, trying to save her life.

"Oh, who is she?" I asked the Judge calmly, as if she was a simple annoyance.

"I don't know—she's just an innocent woman," she replied pleadingly.

"Does she know the door is locked?"

"Leave her alone," the Judge said sternly as I stood up and began to step away from behind the bar.

"You'll be quiet, or I'll silence you too," I shouted back at her, and I stopped to face her before I continued to walk away.

"Does no one have a gun?" the Judge screamed to the people around her. I lifted the guns from the police men that lay cold on the ground.

"Guns make far too much noise. I won't allow them in here."

"That is not for you to decide!" Price screamed. He was standing to my right as I passed. I sighed and spoke softly.

"You have helped me get this far, Jim Price, and believe me, I am very grateful. But I don't need your legal opinion any more. I don't think it matters much now, do you?" I asked as I emptied the bullets from the gun, and threw the empty barrels on the desk that I had been seated behind only minutes before. I put the bullets in my pocket and said, "I have the power now. What you believe or think is of no concern to me. Your advice to me is like these guns—empty and useless."

I walked to the door, and my pace was slower than the frantic footsteps of the woman on the hollow wooden stairs; she had managed to break loose from the crowd. When she came to the curve on the stairs that led her to the ground floor, she met me waiting for her with a smile. She gasped in fear, and began to frantically retreat.

"Don't do that," I said calmly. My mellow voice rang clearly in her ears, and her face softened a little. I extended my hand towards her. "Come closer to me," I said in a whisper. Slowly, her feet began to descend the steps. Her eyes were locked on me, and she moved seamlessly from the steps on to the floor where I stood.

Her fingers touched mine, and slowly she moved her delicate touch over my hand, until I pulled her towards me. The rest of the room was in silence, watching with a frightened anticipation. Her eyes were large and brown. Tears still fell from her eyes, even though they were calm. I saw her fall into a trance as she lost herself in my gaze.

"You're beautiful," she whispered as her eyes scanned each part of my face. I placed my right hand on her waist and pulled her closer to me. I could feel her breath on my neck as she looked up to meet my eyes. The room around us became a haze and there was only the two of us, a similar experience to the short conversation Mr. Price and I had shared, only this time there was passion between us—a definite excitement in the air that surrounded us. She was completely transfixed with me. I smiled as her mouth kissed my neck.

"Are you scared?" I whispered in her ear.

"Yes," she answered plainly as her parched lips opened again.

"Good," I said as I moved my right hand along her body, moving my hand upwards over her curves that extended from her waist. My fingers swept along her neck, and tightened when they felt her blood pulsate under her skin. She looked at me, a frightened gaze swept over her eyes, and the trust that was once there vanished. I tightened my grip as she broke the connection between our hands. My free hand joined the other in silencing her.

"You shouldn't have screamed. You're so beautiful. It's a shame," I said as I kissed her once rosy lips, now fading in colour. Her hands were on my chest, trying to push me away, and with every failed attempt, a tear fell from her closing eyes.

"Have his demands met, Peter. He killed five people in that Courtroom," the Supervisor said, as he buried his head in his hands.

"But, Sir, do you think we should have another hearing before we sentence him?"

Peter Wright asked. Wright was a former fellow lawyer of Jim Price.

"Are you stupid?"

"No."

"You could have fooled me," the Supervisor said with a sarcastic laugh. "Are *you* going to represent him? What Judge do you think will go near this case? He killed the Judge who ruled in *favour* of him for goodness sake, what do you think he'll do to the Judge who finds him guilty? He killed the last and only Lawyer who would represent him, and it was entirely *my* fault."

"Sir, it wasn't your fault," said Wright, as he took a step closer to his boss.

"Don't try to console me, Peter. I persuaded Jim to take this case, and as a result of me, he's d—dead!" He threw his head into his hands and pushed his fingers into his closed eyes in anger.

"Okay, sir. I'll make sure his demands are met. He should be killed for what he's done!"

"You *think* so?" the Supervisor asked. "I'd kill him with my bare hands if I ever laid eyes on him again."

As Peter left his Superior's office, wails were heard through the glass panel of his door. Wails of woe and fury echoed through the corridors, and a silence penetrated the hearts of Jim Price's former colleagues.

Chapter Three

St. Marlon's psychiatric hospital was situated in Storncellak, in the far Northern regions of Scotland, by the coast. It was a converted derelict castle made of harsh and abrasive weathered stone that stood on a hill at the edge of the sea; far from civilisation and isolated by an overgrown forest. It was the perfect place to send Norton. Rupert had taken complete charge over Robert by the time of his arrival. As was expected, there was a slight problem with his presence there: the majority of the Nurses and Doctors refused to treat him.

Shaw was a tall and broad man. He was sturdy in both physical and inner character. He was a man of sixty-five and he had been thinking of retiring for many years, but now it wasn't a case of what age he was, or how long he had worked there for, it was the problem of who would be able to treat Norton after he was gone.

"No, I will not treat him," Nurse Cable said defiantly, trying to remain as reserved as possible. She stumbled away from the Chief Doctor who stood facing her with a stern expression on his face.

"This is your job. He is not a well man and it is your duty to treat him."

"I don't care. I will not be *silenced*—as he calls it. I refuse to be in a cell alone with him."

"Will no one treat him?" Doctor Shaw asked his staff as he addressed them in the conference room.

"No," the staff unanimously answered Shaw.

"This is a disgrace. Not one of you will treat him and therefore I have no choice but to call in experts from London. He has been here for ten years—he's been here longer than some of you. You knew he was here when you applied for the job, so has the dangerous excitement worn off?" Shaw bellowed and he turned on his heels and began to march towards the door.

"Remind us, Doctor, why you cannot treat him any more?" Nurse Cable asked, furious at being shouted at in front of her colleagues. Shaw turned slightly and paused, taking a deep breath before speaking. Nurse Cable had the capability of attacking people with her words with such ease that one could come to no other conclusion than she was a wicked and vicious woman, if one was to come into close contact with her.

"I have worked with him since he has been here. I have worked with him so often that he is comfortable around me; he considers us to be friends. He no longer fears the needles if I bring them or the foul medicine he has to take religiously, and that, staff, is never a good thing, especially with a mind like his," he said quietly and his age suddenly showed in his eyes. He walked to the door and closed it after him, leaving the remaining members of staff feeling anxious and circumspect.

"Hello Doctor," I said as I heard the familiar footsteps outside my door. The iron slide in the door opened and his eyes fell on me. It closed again and the lock of the door was opened with the scraping sound of old keys. The door screamed slowly as it opened and I winced as it rang through my mind. I hated noise, I didn't object to sound, but brutal noise irritated and angered me, as it unsettled the blissful Silence in my mind. "The rule still stands, Doctor. Have you forgotten?" I looked down at his shoes and nodded for them to be removed. Shaw slipped off his cotton white shoes and tossed them outside the door before the screaming door found its place within the doorframe again. I shivered with disgust as I thought of his shoes. Shaw looked at me and sat down opposite me.

"The shoes still annoy you?"

"It's not a phobia, I'm not afraid of shoes, I just hate what they conceal. The feet are the second most beautiful part of the body, second to the eyes of course. One can tell almost anything about a person by looking at their feet. It's how I judge people, to see if they are trustworthy or not, as you already know." I smiled slightly at Shaw as he nodded, remembering the discussion we had had concerning this many years ago.

"Do you know that no one will treat you?"

"Yes, I gathered that. I've only ever been treated by you but I know there are others."

"You are still very perceptive I see."

"I see you still underestimate me, Doctor," I said with a slight smile and Shaw looked at me nervously. "But don't worry, I prefer to be underestimated, it gives the air of surprise when my talents will be truly recognised."

"Do you plan to unveil your talents to the world soon?"

"Yes, but it will be after your time."

"I am only sixty-five; you will have to wait some time," Shaw gave a little chuckle. I remained silent, a small grin emerging from the side of my mouth. I could see Shaw's eyes widen and he looked sternly at me. His laughter lines smoothed out as his complexion turning paler and his expression worrisome.

"Yes. It will still be after your time," I said in a nonchalant manner.

"Why?" Shaw asked, a frightened curiosity filtering through his eyes.

"You would be the only one who could stop me."

"Me?" Shaw asked, a mesmerized expression dawning on his face, almost one of pride.

"Yes, it could only be you," I answered and stood up to my full height. Shaw scrambled to his feet and donned the same composure.

"Are you ready?" Shaw asked, putting his hand in his pocket.

"Let's just do it, I have to keep Robert at bay, he keeps trying to surface," I said as I closed my eyes and leant against the wall, holding out my left fore arm to Shaw. I had so much adrenaline in my veins that Shaw had never once needed to strap my arm to raise a vein; they were all prominent on my arms and legs. The needle penetrated my skin and I felt my brain tense as the medicine surged through my body.

When Shaw reached his warm carpeted office he slid off his shoes and pushed his toes into the carpet. It hugged his toes and warmed them after the cold stone floor of Norton's cell. He leant back in his chair and thought of what Norton had said. He became slightly worried that he would kill him. It had always been a possible scenario, but since they had made their relationship almost one of friendship, that possibility had seemed to linger elsewhere than in the forefront of Shaw's mind. But now it resurfaced with vengeance, and he wondered if he should have a plan, as Norton obviously did. His eyes widened as he dwelled on the idea, then shook his head, refusing to remain on that thought for too long; it was too depressing a subject to linger on for too long, for it would be likely to consume one's own mind. He opened his drawer and took out an address book. He found the telephone number of London's

18

Head Psychiatric Hospital and dialled the number. He hoped they would be able to send members of staff within the week, his mind was beginning to become paranoid and worried, and he thought of how much longer he would be able to remain sane in the presence of the most insane schizophrenic patient the world had ever known.

Chapter Four

Shaw knew that he would have to persuade his staff to at least walk past the cell that held the most vicious, yet the most fascinating, psychopath that had met the walls of St. Marlon's. He didn't want the London officials thinking they couldn't do their jobs *at all—* he wouldn't allow that. *Sooner or later they're going to have to deal with him; I will not have them embarrassing me and this hospital.* With a nod and a brisk stride, he walked towards the staff room where all the staff were eating and having their tea breaks before resigning back to the jobs they were all reluctant to continue.

The members of staff jumped as the door flung open. Shaw greeted them with his usual stern and sharp expression. The conversations were interrupted by the courteous acknowledgements from his inferiors. The Boss always had an air of expertise, and everyone marvelled at his bravery in dealing with Norton. He was the one patient everyone refused to treat, even though there was an air of mystery surrounding the darkened walls that led to the silent and ominous cell that inhabited him. Yet their curiosity never matched their fear, and they kept clear of that route.

"Right, listen up all of you. You have disgraced this hospital enough, and I will not let it continue in the presence of the London crew. I have rung them and they are sending three men to deal with Norton because you cannot. I should sack every one of you this instant. Show that you are capable of doing the jobs you were once trained to do and you might be able to keep them. Some one work with the patient you all have neglected for so long. I expect to see at least one of you doing their job and dealing with Norton tonight," he said sternly before he turned swiftly and walked out of the room, leaving the Nurses and Doctors pale faced and anxious.

I heard the usual set of footsteps as they echoed through the lonely corridor outside my cell. As I listened, my eras detected the distinct sound of Shaw's heart beating faster than his usual rhythm. What I had said to him must have affected him on some level. I was glad it did affect him, because I hadn't been witness to anyone being scared of me in ten years. I knew the others were scared of me, but my ears had never listened to their frightened heartbeats whispering from within their cages; the desperate eyes of a pleading soul hadn't met my gaze in too long; the taste of death hadn't rested upon my body like a blanket of comfort in longer than I cared to remember. However, that was about to change, and Shaw's perception of his death was about to change too.

I listened to him as he kicked off his shoes and followed the ritual of opening the iron slide and resting his eyes on my distant position before entering. A small smile grew from the corners of my mouth as I knew his end was approaching. As I wondered about what his deathly silence would sound and feel like, I was overcome with excitement. I realized I hadn't silenced any one in ten years, and I had almost forgotten what the sweet taste of power and satisfaction tasted like.

"Good evening Norton," Shaw said and he nodded, watching me, his eyes filled with a dubious and untrusting gaze, even after all this time.

"Why are you here, Doctor? You normally only see me twice a day and your hour of expected arrival has not yet dawned," I asked as I smiled and indicated for him to make himself comfortable in his usual sitting space opposite me on the stone floor.

"How was your dinner earlier?" Shaw asked, and his small talk began.

"Oh it was perfect, cheese, bread and a few slices of barely cooked ham; who could ask for more?" I smirked slightly from the corner of my mouth and Shaw looked at me seriously.

"We have become close over your time here, Norton, and I value the trust you have placed in me, but I am sorry to say that my visits cannot continue. As you know, the other members of staff are incredibly wary of you, and I think the time has come for you and them to become acquainted. You will be eating in the Cafeteria with the rest of the patients from now on, Norton, and I will not be giving you your medication any longer, it will be given to you by one of the Nurses or one of the Doctors, perhaps even both."

"That's not a problem, Shaw."

"Good. I am disappointed that it has come to this, I thoroughly enjoyed analyzing your intelligent and marvellous persona."

"Flattery is always appreciated, but there is no need to soften the news of your departure from my presence. As devastating as it is, I've known you would be leaving me for some time now, so I have come to accept the idea. I have made sure that your departure from me will be as smooth and as soft as possible, and I have decided that it will be me who will have the honour of seeing you off."

"What are you talking about? There is no need for anything out of the ordinary, Norton," Shaw said with a nervous edge to his voice. I could see the sudden surge of adrenaline as it powered through his body, because his eyes reacted and his body forced him up against the wall. His hand reached into his pocket, where he kept the emergency supply of a sedative.

"There's no need to use that," I said, as I walked slowly towards Shaw, my height bearing down on his five foot seven frame. "Calm down and accept me."

Shaw stuttered as he eyed the door, hoping an escape would appear. His eyes bulged as my shadow descended on him. The scream that uttered from him was horrific to my ears, and I wrapped my fingers around his neck. The scream muffled in the dense Silence that hung in my lair, built up over the many years of my residency.

The fear spread through him almost faster than the adrenaline had. His eyes filled with tears and his eyebrows furrowed, a silent plead for mercy spreading upon his face. The colour of his skin around his eyes and mouth began to deepen in the shadows as the blood surged past my fingers; the thick viscous liquid slowly beginning to slow.

His fingers lost their energy as they clawed unsuccessfully at mine. I held his body as it began to falter, my left arm bearing the weight of the man who had befriended me and now had to die for my plan to be successfully completed. He challenged me with one final burst of life, but faltered more so after, until I was holding him in my arms, cradling him as my hand silenced him and took away the voice that had defended me for so long.

The Silence that engulfed me after his final breath was overwhelming. I sat in the Silence of death as it clung to my heart and made my chest heave as it tried to regulate a beat. My body's rhythm echoed loudly in my ears and in my chest, banging against my rib cage like a furious and untamed animal.

Tears flowed from my eyes, but the emotion that overwhelmed me was not mine, it was Robert's.

"Get back now," I whispered to Robert. He had not surfaced in ten years, and he was not going to surface now and spoil everything I had planned and worked for.

You killed him! He was the only one who listened to us.

He never listened to you.

You know I speak out when you are asleep, he has my words, thoughts and feelings written down and hidden, you murdered the only one who had any time for us; he slept when we didn't need him, he sat outside that cell all night, every night, listening to me, talking and consoling me. I hate you!

Shut up and keep dormant. That's the only way I like you, when you're out of the way. I took over and you agreed to it, so tough, there's nothing you can do about it. I'm the stronger one and you'll thank me like you thanked me before. You need my power and you know it. Now haunt the crevices of the mind where you belong and don't bother me any more. I have work to do.

The wailing sobs of Robert ceased after a while and I shook his words from my conscience. His appearance in my mind was becoming more frequent and I knew it was only a matter of time before he awoke completely from the dormant regions of my mind. Even though Robert had surfaced the emotion that had overcome me, I felt an emotion that I knew was my own. I felt respect for the aged man whose body was limp and motionless on the stone floor beside me—pale faced and ghostly. I looked through the bars of my cell, which were rusted and old, and saw the moon make more of its journey through the night sky. As the low moon-beams reached my gaze, I stood up and walked back into the darkness opposite and watched as Shaw's dark mass was slowly illuminated by a silver glow of Silence—a heavenly repose to a frightful, yet necessary, death.

Chapter Five

A tension filled the staff room where Shaw's former colleagues stood. They had thrown away their food, unable to fathom a meal after being confronted with the news that one, or two, of them would have to prepare themselves to meet the darkness that they had avoided successfully for so long.

Keelin Hogan was a young woman, whose curiosity had led her in the direction of Norton's cell before. She had remained awake throughout that particular night, thinking of the dangerous allure that spun like a spider's web from the sensuous silence that draped the corridor that only Norton inhabited. A frightened, yet excited, girl of twenty-six was about to feed her fantasy, but this time she would *see* the man who had sparked such electrifying feelings. *When a man is so dangerous and dark, there comes a point where your fright turns to fancy.* She had justified her desire many times before to her conscience, and the mysterious man, who she had only seen in black and white photos in the newspapers, was about to become more real than she could ever have hoped for.

"I'll treat him," Keelin said and her voice sounded a little hoarse from restraining an excited scream. However, the tone in her voice was perceived as terror, and the male Doctors had a sudden sense of bravery, sparked by her innocent, yet strikingly beautiful, features.

"It is quite alright, Keelin, I shall deal with him tonight," said Paul Newdeck, a highly respected male Doctor.

"No. This is my job and all of you have had some encounter with Norton. You were all here ten years ago, I wasn't, and I want to have the experience of treating him."

Dubious, yet respectful, stares met hers as she looked around the room, as she attempted to convince her co-workers that this was her choice and final decision.

"I think I should go with you," Paul said, his broad physique standing tall like a Roman warrior.

"I think I am quite capable of dealing with Norton myself, Paul," she said, as she gave him a stern look, and Paul's strong physique lessened under her stare. "A woman is just as capable of doing a man's job, Paul—Doctor Newdeck."

"Hey, I never said you weren't capable of doing anything. I merely thought you might need assistance."

"Why would I need assistance? Shaw said he would see one of us up there, so I presume that means he'll be there, what do you think?" she asked defiantly and she tilted her head in an almost patronizing manner. This was enough to stir fury in Paul and he stood silently, glaring into her face, before reseating himself on the sofa behind him.

"Go on then, Keelin, before you change your mind," Paul said, folding his arms and smirking slightly. Keelin rolled her eyes at him, and tossed her long brown hair in his direction before walking confidently through the large door that faced them.

"I see you and Keelin haven't sorted things out then, Paul?" Nurse Angelina Ronston said, her deep, yet brittle, voice slithering its way to Paul's ears. He looked at her and spoke nonchalantly.

"Did you like the dig I made at her at the end?" he asked. He repositioned himself on the cushions and his pomp returned.

"Yeah, she's as fickle as they come, Paul. You're better off without her."

"You still seem protective of her, Paul. It's as clear as day she still isn't out of your system," Karen, another Nurse, said, as she turned to the kitchenette to prepare a pot of tea.

"I can't help it. I've loved her from the moment I laid eyes on her, and it's hard seeing that beautiful face every day. How am I supposed to get over her when she's around me all day, every day?"

"Focus your mind on your work," Karen said as she brushed off Paul's immature spiel about love. Karen, at the age of fifty-three, Karen was cynical about devotion of any kind, as her life beyond her work had made her bitter towards it.

"Work is where Keelin is. I mean, we were on and off constantly, she might change her mind again and come back to me."

"Isn't that the reason it's never going to work? There's nothing to build anything on, it's clear she's getting over you. Give her space and stop acting like you're always there to save her, then perhaps her anger will subside," Karen said. Angelina placed one hand on Paul's shoulder, pressing her fingers into his muscle. Angelina had set her eyes on Paul's muscular body since they began working there, and their flirting had been making great progress, until Keelin had appeared, and Angelina was thrown out of the picture..

A nervous anticipation swept through Keelin as she walked through the stone corridors, which were dark with the deepening night. She wrapped her fingers around the rusting banister rails as they ascended through spiral staircases, leading to the top floor of the hospital.

When she reached the last few steps, the Silence that engulfed her made her heart doubtful of her idea to approach his cell door. As she stood motionless at the top of the stairway, her mind and heart telling her to do opposite things, she tried to decide what she was to do. Without another thought, an answer came to her from the darkness beyond—it was encouraging her and attracting her into the deeper realms with tendrils of black beckoning her into the shadows. The shadows from the ceiling and the penetrating Silence clung to the sea breeze that was blowing through Keelin's long, brown and delicate hair, which made her step closer to him. She smiled as her heart pounded faster as she took the steps towards his cell.

The shoes Keelin saw startled her slightly at first, but she was not overly surprised—she knew Shaw couldn't bear the frustration of sitting outside Norton's cell, not when he could be talking to the most fascinating mind he had ever studied, especially when he knew he would have to keep away from him soon.

"Doctor Shaw? It's Keelin Hogan," she said. Her voice was engulfed by the Silence and she doubted if Shaw would have heard her. Slowly, she placed her quivering left hand on the metal door in front of her. As her fingertips rested on the cold door, the feeling sent a shiver of anticipation through her body.

The coldness of the metal door ran up and down her spine, and she could hear movement from inside. With a thrill she had never experienced before she raised her right hand. Her fingers followed the metal upwards to the sliding iron grate that would illuminate inside to her. She wrapped her thumb and index finger around the small latch that faced her, and she slowly began to push it to her left. She didn't know if she was breathing or not, all her energy, life and consciousness was directed at who was behind that door. Fear engulfed her, but it vanished instantly, and a sheer sense of delight and awe spread through her, when she saw him facing her—a startled expression mirrored in his green eyes, which dissolved to an almost mesmerized gaze.

Chapter Six

I sat and listened to the rhythmic rush of the waves as they gently caressed the sand on the shore beyond the restricting walls. As I listened I heard something that normally didn't reach my ears—a new set of footsteps. My eyes instantly moved to Shaw and I put my arms under his, hoisting him up, before dragging him into the darkest corner of my confined space.

I heard the footsteps gather and wade through the Silence that lingered in my corridor, and I heard them become slower as they found their place outside my door. A warm and mysterious energy filtered through the metal door. My anticipation raced, as did my heart, and as I listened I found that the heart outside requited mine. I walked curiously over to the door and stood facing the iron grid, waiting for eyes to meet mine. I heard the soft touch of delicate fingers on the film of silence that veiled the door; and I knew it was a woman. Her other hand glided along the metal noiselessly, finding its place on the grid separating us. The slow and heavy iron latch opened.

Through the grey darkness came an array of electrifying blue. Her deep eyes fell on mine and I began to feel something I had never felt before: I wanted her with me; I needed her to be mine. Surprising myself, a strange sense of tranquillity began to ebb and flow through my mind, and I felt Robert awaken. Robert didn't fully appear, but I knew whatever I was feeling was part of the emotional and loving side of my mind. But this was different, because *I* felt it too. Her eyes made me admit it to myself—I wanted her. The feeling was alien to me, yet it was a welcomed stranger. I embraced her glowing skin with my intense gaze. My eyes read hers and I knew she felt the same. I forgot where I was; who I was; why I was here at all. All I knew was that I had to know her.

Green sparkling eyes met Keelin's and all the worry, anxiety and fear washed calmly from her and was replaced with a blissful wanting of the man behind the door. She focused on his steady eyes, unblinking and unwavering, and knew she had to have him. She had to know him. Her fingers blindly fell on the many metal keys that weighed down her right pocket. Their eyes were still mesmerized with the other's faces. Then he spoke.

"Before you come in, take off your shoes. I need to know you," he said. His voice was deep and mellow and it reverberated in Keelin's ears and chest, sending a sensuous rush through her body. She placed her toes on the back of each heel and kicked off the white pumps that cushioned her feet. She watched as his eyes began to retreat further into the room and she knew he was awaiting her presence.

Averting her eyes from where they had been transfixed, she closed the iron grid and looked down at the keys that hung in her fingers. Her fingers fumbled for the key that had a red plastic coating (red for warning) and proceeded to push it into the small hole in the door. Her hand turned it with a force she had not expected to need, and pulled it out again. She placed her keys back in her pocket and put both her hands on the metal door handle, which was positioned at waist height.

The door gently opened, and the artificial light from outside filtered through the door, expanding on the floor as it opened further. She closed the door behind her and put her stood with her back against the door. Her chest heaved; her eyes were wide; her pupils were dilated as they tried to adjust to the darkness.

I walked back to where the moon beams touched the wall. Her ears pricked as she heard me in the darkness. After a few moments her eyes adjusted and they found me. Her whole body relaxed as she surrendered to me, a small smile emerging from the corners of her cherry coloured lips. Shaw remained in the corner, a dark shadow in a mass of darkness that accumulated at the corners. Keelin seemed unaware that his dead body lay near her; all her focus was on me and she seemed to have forgotten all about his pair of shoes that sat outside the door. The complete focus of her mind was on me and I was beginning to feel the same way.

I looked down at her feet. She had taken her shoes off without question, showing she had nothing to hide. I needed to see her walk towards me, in order to see if she would falter and if she could be trusted completely. She seemed to read my mind, and my eyes fell on hers as she began to glide through the darkness. My gaze followed the curves of her body. The movement of her hips and waist with each step she took was hypnotic. I followed her long legs to the ground and I watched as her delicate feet moved. Snowy white ankles led to her slender, feminine feet that were draped in soft, white, cotton socks. Her feet had a strong walk—a definite purpose and stride. She did not threaten me, and I knew I could trust her.

Passion and desire surged through me as she whispered my name through the dark air. I could feel Robert twitch and for the first time since our union ten years ago, we felt like one being. His feelings influenced mine, and mine his. Lust poured in through my eyes as I watched the moonbeams fall on her glistening hair; her perfect complexion; her angel-like body. Her eyes twinkled in the moonbeams as the dust motes danced around her, moving and swaying with each passing movement. I was completely besotted with her, and I could tell she requited my new found obsession.

She didn't stop walking until our bodies touched. Her breathing was shallow. I felt her chest heave quickly as it pressed against mine. Our eyes gazed into each other's. An excitement burned inside me and it raged through my body and through to my fingertips making them move. I was hardly aware that my arms were moving, yet I did not object to their motion. My fingers of my right hand followed her arm up towards her shoulder, and they positioned themselves over her long and soft neck, until they curved over her jaw and felt the soft skin on her face. My left hand followed the curves of her hips, meandering with the contours of her goddess-like figure. Her waist was where my hand decided to remain. I felt her hips below my hand, and I felt her ribcage begin another meander above. Her eyes closed as my right hand reached the back of her neck, sending a chill through her spine. When she opened them again, mine were closer to hers than before. Our lips were nearly touching; our noses align with each other's.

Her eyes fell to my lips and I watched as they proceeded to assess every feature of my face. I felt her fingers gently progress across my hips as they glided up towards my waist. She moved her hands and they nestled by my mid-drift— one on my ribs that protruded slightly, and the other on my abdomen, which was hard and sturdy. I rippled my fingers at the back of her neck, and her pony tail brushed against them as it draped down her back. She smiled slightly and her eyes glistened with excitement. As she closed her eyes slightly, I felt her body press ever so slightly harder against mine.

30

I tilted my head slightly and moved my lips closer to hers. When we touched, an overwhelming sense of delight race through me. I felt it surge through her too, as she held me tighter, and I held her closer. My left hand moved from her waist to her back and I pressed her body even closer to mine as I tore the ribbon from its assigned place, which had held her straight hair in a neat design. Her fringe fell forward; her long hair fell on to my chest as it framed her face. My fingers ran through her silky hair and our breathing became shallower, more intense as the passion grew from within us.

I moved her to the wall and her back pressed against the wall where mine had just been. I kissed her neck and felt her body as she kissed me. My lips travelled back to hers and then she suddenly froze. Her lips did not reciprocate the kisses mine gave; her hands fell from me and moved to her face to cover her mouth; her eyes were no longer bright with passion, but rather surged with a fear that I had seen in Shaw's eyes. Then it dawned on me.

Her eyes were fixed on the corner behind me—on the darkened mass that she recognized as her Boss. I could feel a wrenching motion start from her stomach, and I took hold of her and carried her to the opposite corner of the room. Tears grew in her eyes and poured from them as she gasped for breath through every sob. Her knees buckled and I sat her down with me in the darkness, holding her shaking body. I knew that no one would hear her sorrowful cries from my lonely and deserted corridor. My arms tried to wrap around her, but the second I had done so she crawled away from me with frightened eyes—it had only dawned on her in that second that she was in the arms of the man who had murdered her friend and colleague. She couldn't manage to find her feet, so instead she grabbled at the floor, furiously attempting to move closer to the figure that lay in the corner opposite.

"Shaw…" she moaned through tears. She sat on her knees, watching and nudging Shaw with her hands, trying to determine if he was actually dead or not.

For minutes the only sound that was heard was the soft regretful sobs that poured from the young girl opposite me. I knew she was in her twenties, but looking at her reminded me of myself when I was a child—lonely and sore from pain. Then, suddenly, venom surged within her, and that was all she knew. For the first time in my new and transformed life, I was afraid of someone. Her bloodshot eyes threw daggers at me as she jerked her head around to look at me. I put my hands on the wall behind me and hoisted myself up. I was six foot three, and she was approximately five foot seven, but I felt miniscule under her stares. An irrational fear surged through me. I knew I could win any fight and I knew I could kill her if I wanted to— if I had to. But there was a difference this time—I knew I *wasn't* going to kill her, even if that meant I had to die.

She found her feet through the strength the anger gave her and she charged at me. As she hurled her body at me, I could do nothing. Her legs were instantaneously wrapped around my waist and her hands were clenched at my throat. I tried to pry her from me, but she had an unwavering vengeance. As I began to become overwhelmed, I fell to my knees and fell on top of her. My fingers tore at her hair and I bit at her neck, trying to make her stop. Her eyes were squinted and focused with rage as her nails dug into my skin.

"Stop it, you wicked thing," I said hoarsely as I started to feel the air around me become heavy and almost unbreathable.

"I am not the wicked one—you murderer."

"You knew I was one before…before…" A darkness began to filter through my mind, and I knew I was about to become unconscious. "Don't kill me…" I said just as I felt myself fall limp around her, and I felt her scurry from underneath me. The Silence took over and all energy left my muscles. The only thing I heard was the slowing pulse of my heart in my ears and a distant murmur of a girl calling my name.

Chapter Seven

The sun was just beginning to rise. Its rays lit Keelin's face and she tried not to squint against it. Her body had become numb from the hypnotic sound of the tide as it had filled Keelin's ears while she sat with Norton's limp body in her arms. The cell where she had fought Norton last night didn't bear any illusive marks to indicate what had happened. Shaw's body lay opposite her, unmoved from the previous night. Two pairs of shoes sat beside his body: Shaw's and Keelin's.

Keelin sat with her knees bent slightly, her back against the wall, her face brightened by the dull light of dawn. Her mind flew back to the previous night's happenings for the hundredth time. She hadn't known what to do, so she had decided to wait and see what prospects would reveal themselves to her when a new day dawned. But no new thoughts or decisions appeared and all she could do was wait for Norton to regain consciousness.

A twitch from the body in her arms averted her eyes from the bars that kept out the world. She felt guilty for hurting him, yet proud that she had made some attempt to avenge the death of a man who had been like a father to her. She stared at the moving eyes beneath his lids, and waited for them to open—and find their attacker. She felt afraid that he would wreak havoc on her and kill her just like he had killed the only man who had ever respected him. All night she hadn't been able to fathom his reasons and she had to admit, she was intrigued to listen to them—if she would get the chance to live that long.

The darkness seemed to lift from within my mind and I could see the inside redness of my eyelids as light poured through the thin skin. Consciousness found me then and I remembered what had happened. I didn't want to open my eyes because I didn't want to see who Keelin had handed me over to and what was to become of me now that I had killed an Official. But as those thoughts dissipated, I felt strength surround me and I became aware that some-one was holding me. My eyes opened and I saw long brown hair draped over a shoulder, supporting an arm that was supporting me. I followed the features I recognized and then I found her face. Disorientation vanished suddenly and my instincts took control of me. I leapt from her arms and stumbled away from her to the window. The fresh sea breeze hit my face and I was thankful I hadn't died— not for the lack of trying on her part. But my eyes couldn't part from her. I stared at the beautiful woman with tear stained cheeks sitting by the wall, her legs outstretched, her arms limply placed by her side, and her eyes focused on me. I wanted desperately to kiss her, but I mustered all the strength I had and kept my distance.

"What the hell did you try to kill me for?"

"You killed Shaw."

"Yes, I know I did. It wasn't an easy thing to do but I had to do it."

"No you didn't," she said as her eyes squinted and her eyebrows furrowed.

"What the hell do you know? You don't know anything about me! You know my files and my recorded self, but only Shaw knew something of the real me. I never met you before until last night—you were too preoccupied with the simple patients to bother with me!"

"You're talking as if you know everything about *me*. I started working here nine years ago to get *closer* to you. You were the most fascinating case I had ever set my eyes on, and I wanted you the second I laid my eyes on your picture—I loved you the second I wanted you. But you didn't even see me; you were too preoccupied with killing the people who got close to you." She stood up and pointed at her late Boss, sitting with a lolled head, as if asleep.

"If you loved me then why did you try to kill me?"

"If you loved Shaw, then why did you kill him?"

"Just stop it. You don't know what I'm planning to do. I'm planning something and Shaw would have been the only one who could have stopped me."

"Well if that's what you're going to do to the people who can stop you from doing things, then I had better get out of your way," she said as she smirked slightly and tossed her hair. Standing now, she began to walk to the door.

"Don't leave, please," I said. An unusual fear poisoned me, as if I was actually afraid that I had lost her. "You were stronger than me last night. If you stand in my way of freedom then I *will* kill you. I—I—I love you, that is why I didn't kill you last night."

"I love you. That was why *I* didn't kill *you* last night."

We stared at each other for a few seconds. I slid down the wall and sat down on the stone floor. Keelin remained standing.

"Come and sit with me," I said, hoping she would. She bent to the floor and retrieved the ribbon and then turned away from me. Her delicate hands gathered all her hair and tied the ribbon around it, keeping it in place.

"Will you tell me everything?" she asked as she played with her hair, and she turned to face me again. "I want to understand you. I'm comple*tely* obsessed with *every*thing about you. I'm not afraid of you any more. I love you, and I choose you, over all the rest."

She smiled and put her hands in the pockets of her blue cotton pinafore. I smiled back, and I glanced once more at her feet, felt one more pang of a deep obsession that I knew was love, and spoke truthfully.

"I will tell you everything if you promise to love me implicitly. Will you only be mine?" I asked and looked hopefully at her. She looked at Shaw and then back at me.

"I will fight for you. I will stick by you, because I have been waiting to be with you for ten years. I love you."

I chose to trust her, because I saw something of myself in her: her strength; her fearlessness; her devotion to something her heart tells her to be true, even though the rest of the world frowns upon it as inviolable and outlandish. It was when she sat in my arms and listened with fascination that I realized my plans were going to change. I knew that my original plan of silencing the disrespectful inhabitants of the world was no longer my priority. I was no longer just in the fight for Silence, I was in the fight for Silence, tranquillity and, ultimately, Keelin.

Chapter Eight

The morning was rapidly gaining as we talked. I felt like I knew her
more than I had known anyone, even Shaw. She listened, transfixed, as
I told her of my new plan, of my quest to silence those that prevent
tranquillity and a quiet life to be one with the earth. The need for
vengeance and revenge pulsed through me as I talked of my parents,
exactly what had happened with them, the Courtroom and how my life
had amounted to this—a trapped and isolated mind and heart, consoled
only by the friendly Silence that accompanied me through my
treacherous journey. The Silence had been my only true friend...until
now.

"I will help you," Keelin said, excitement emerging on her face
through a smile.

"Are you sure?"

"I love you. I am sure. I have waited so long to be with you, no
one else compares to you now, Norton, you are my life, and I will die
trying to save you—before it is too late."

"Thank you Keelin. I never expected this off anyone, I thought
everyone would be against me, but you are like me, you are mine.
Thank you for helping me."

Having spent so much time being deprived of a life that I could
be in control of had left my heart weakened. I was beginning to lose the
strength I once had, and I refused to spend any more time trapped in a
cell, confined to a small breath of fresh air every time the wind blew
east. I knew I had to fulfil my ambition of being free for the remainder
of my time, whether that be in the forest, on the sea shore or in a small
house on a deserted land, away from dogmatic rules, questioning glares,
medication and control. I had to be in control of something, and my

death was something that I *had* to take control of. There was nothing left to do but start the fight.

"I suppose I will find it hard to see some-one die?"

"It always is, but don't be afraid, strength and power come to you when you need them most, like last night."

She lifted her eyes to mine and I saw guilt in her expression. I smiled softly and leant towards her, reaching out to her lips with mine. She met mine with the softest touch, which turned into a complete embrace.

"My shift starts at nine..." she said as she trailed the kiss off, wishing it didn't have to end. I knew that our fight had to begin today, and so I began thinking.

"Who is the most superior after Shaw?"

"That would be Doctor Clarine."

"Who is that?"

"She ignores everyone, but it's great to see she is afraid of you too. There's something so *sexy* about a dangerous man," she said and I noticed her pupil's dilate as she assessed my rugged features: my green eyes, my untamed hair, my broad and built physique.

"Bring her to me," I said. Keelin's flirtatious glare cut off as I spoke.

"What? She'll see Shaw. Besides, she wouldn't listen to me even if it was something important."

"Even if it was *really* important?"

Her expression changed and I knew she understood what I was suggesting.

"Okay. I'll do it. I hope it works." She walked over to her shoes and slid her dainty feet into them, fixed them at her heels with her fingers and walked back to where I was sitting. "Aren't you going to stand up and gave me a kiss for good luck?" She smirked and delicately placed her hand out to me. I took hold of it and stood up. I swung her around with ease and then gently tilted her back so that her weight was supported in my arms. Her long hair flowed from the ribbon like silk. She smiled and as I leant in to meet her lips, I knew I had found some one so special, so dangerously perfect for me and so strikingly beautiful, and for the first time in my entire life, I was actually happy to be me.

Keelin walked with a skip in her step through the corridors towards the main sector of the building where Clarine's office was. Her long hair swayed from side to side and she noticed she had adopted a delicate strut that she had not modelled before she had kissed her out-of-bounds man. Shivers went through her spine as she remembered the kisses, his body, even the fighting sent a sensuous hunger surging through her—she had a new found dangerous appetite. She had to think of Shaw's lonely body to wipe the smile from her face before knocking on Clarine's door.

"Yes?"

The voice was quick to respond to her knock, and it sounded impatient. Keelin turned the handle and opened the wooden door. Her heart began to beat faster and fear swept through her as she saw Paul standing at Clarine's desk, both his hands on the wood, wearing a stern and red faced complexion. He looked at Keelin and rolled his eyes, obviously not happy to see her.

"Speak of the devil," Paul said and his pompous and arrogant tone was unmistakable. "I was just talking about you to Doctor Clarine."

"It's Doctor Clarine Johnston to you," she said sternly as she stood up from her black leather chair and her tall and thin body levelled with Paul's height. Keelin didn't know how she was going to convince Clarine with her story when Paul's criticizing and obnoxious comments were sure to upset the original plan. She hated Paul, but at this moment, she hated him more than she had hated anyone. *Why can't he just back off? How dare he criticize me to Clarine. The arrogant, sickening and disgusting pig!*

Paul stepped aside and sat down in the blue chair and crossed his legs, assessing the situation like some-one with actual intellect. Keelin gave him a cold glance and then proceeded to step closer to Clarine's desk. Clarine still had her eyes fixed on Paul and anger still resided in them as she tore them away and rested them on Keelin.

"Doctor Johnston, I really need to talk to you. It's a private and urgent matter."

"What's wrong?" Paul asked, his curious voice reaching from behind her. Keelin remained still but addressed Paul with a sharp tone.

"If it concerned you, I would have invited you into the conversation."

Keelin heard a small snort erupt from behind her and she tried to remain calm and focused on Clarine's reaction.

"Go and see Doctor Shaw, he is your Boss and I have far too much paper work to do," she said with a finality that made Keelin's stomach fall. She sat down and licked her index finger as she flicked through files and sighed. She looked up at Keelin with a questioning look, as if to say *why are you still here?* Keelin could feel Paul's smug eyes glare and burn into her back. She had not expected Clarine to take much notice of her, but with Paul sitting behind her the outcome of success seemed even bleaker than before. Keelin stepped closer so that she could feel the wood of the table against her legs.

"What if it was a *very* important matter?"

"I would say the same thing, go and see Doctor Shaw."

"What if it concerned Doctor Shaw?" Keelin asked, and she knew she had struck a weak point. She knew she could make the rules now. Clarine had always wanted to take Shaw's place as Chief Doctor, and as she presumed Keelin's topic of conversation was a complaint, she put her files to one side.

"Then of course I will listen to your matter," she said as she indicated for Keelin to have a seat to the right of her. Clarine took off her glasses, making her appearance less stern and reproachable. Keelin remained standing, and she knew now was the time to get rid of Paul.

"I will not proceed with my matter until he has left the room."

Keelin could feel the hairs on the back of her neck stand on end and she knew Paul was furious at not knowing information. It had always been one of his dreadfully bad points— he hated not knowing things. Clarine kept her eyes on Keelin, with a slight smile painted on her pale face.

"Leave now, Paul."

"No," Paul said, and a shuffle of feet made Keelin aware that he was standing in objection.

"We will discuss your matter another time."

"I want to hear what she has to say," Paul said, annoyance creeping through his tone. Keelin and Clarine both looked at him sternly. He walked forward and stood beside Keelin. "I want to show you what I mean, Doctor Johnston," he said and he nudged his head slightly in the direction of Keelin.

"I see. Well, your timing may prove to complement you, Nurse Hogan. Pull over those two chairs and we'll listen to whatever you have to say."

Keelin could not believe her ears. She knew there was no point in persisting any further, so with a heavy heart she walked with Paul as they brought two blue chairs over to Clarine's desk.

She knew she had to improvise, and she knew her instincts would guide her in the right direction—they *had* led her to Norton after all.

"I went to the top corridor last night, to treat Norton."

"Yes, I was aware Shaw had told you to get your act together—you plural I mean."

"Yes, well, something strange caught my eye—"

"What?" Paul and Clarine both gasped; their eyes wide and full of suspense.

"Shaw's shoes were outside the door."

"Naturally; you know about the rule that freak has don't you?" Paul asked and Keelin had never felt so much venom rage inside her.

"That was not the strange thing. I called and I received a strange answer telling me to come back later. I obeyed and came back an hour later and his shoes were still outside the room. I called again, and Shaw answered me again, telling me to come back later. I obeyed again, and I came back for the third time. The shoes were still outside. He told me to forget about their meeting tonight and that he had this under control for another night."

"What's strange about that? You know that Shaw is a genius with that beast; he has weird and wonderful ways of dealing with him. What's so strange?" Clarine asked, hoping there was more to my story than that.

"I decided to go back up to the room this morning, because my instincts were telling me that something was wrong, and when I arrived there, both of his shoes were still there, untouched and unmoved from the night before. I called and there was no answer. I knocked and called again, but I became incredibly scared and knew something wasn't right, so that's when I came down here."

"I'll go up and investigate," Paul said standing up, his chest pumped out as if he had gained a kilo of muscle.

"I really think Doctor Clarine should investigate this. It's not for the feint hearted," Keelin said with an almost patronizing tone. She gave him a side glance and watched as his demeanour shrank.

"Then we shall all go," Clarine said, standing up and taking Paul by the arm.

"I didn't want to cause so much trouble," Keelin said and her heart began to drop again. She began praying that a distraction would come and he would be averted. They walked out the door and to Keelin's ultimate gratitude; a possible distraction meandered her way through the corridor.

Keelin had never been so happy to see Angelina. To Keelin's luck, Angelina was looking more ravishing than Keelin had ever seen her. Her long blonde hair blew in the breeze that flew through the corridor, her streamlined body and delicate curves accentuated by her skin tight Nurse's outfit that she had re-stitched to fully flaunt her figure. She held the clip board tight against her chest and when she met them her flirting was enough to cause Keelin to smile slightly at Paul's open mouth.

"Here's the medical bill you wanted Doctor," she said. She licked her finger and latched it on to the first page on her clip board, tearing it off slowly and handing it to Clarine. She looked dangerously at Keelin, and then took a step closer to Paul, and spoke in a sultry tone. "If it's not too much trouble could you get the Vicodin off the top shelf in the Medicine closet, I just can't reach." She smiled and looked at him with wanting eyes.

"That would be no problem at all, Angelina. I'll accompany you right now."

"Oh, that's perfect," Angelina said with exaggerated happiness. Keelin thought she could have said the same thing.

"I thought you were going to accompany us, Paul?" Clarine asked.

"You two are capable enough to handle this on your own," he said as he walked off with Angelina, and she tossed her hair in the gentle breeze.

As Keelin and Clarine walked up the stone steps that led to the top floor, Keelin couldn't help but laugh. She saw something in Clarine that she had never seen before—humour.

"Go on Paul, it's not as if we're confronting a serial killer or anything. I mean, what are men like? A gorgeous woman snaps her fingers and any man runs. With Angelina treating patients I'm surprised most of them haven't died from heart attacks already."

Keelin began to feel very sympathetic towards Clarine because she knew her ultimate fate. She refused to lose her composure, though, she had done everything well so far, and luck had been on her side. Yet she still wanted to tell Clarine to run and get out.

When they neared Norton's door, the breeze that had blown through the corridors beneath them grew colder, and Silence echoed through the walls, filling their ears with nothing but the sound of their own heart beats and nervous footsteps. When they arrived at Norton's door, his scent filled Keelin's nostrils and her doubt was completely replaced with a dangerous and futile wanting—a burning desire for her forbidden man that lay listening on the other side of the door.

Chapter Nine

Clarine looked pale and frightened as they neared Norton's cell. Keelin remembered how she had felt the last time she had walked this path. In her mind she smiled, but her expression was worried and anxious in Clarine's wake. Shaw's shoes were still outside the door, where Keelin had placed them before proceeding with their plan. Keelin watched as the stern, authoritative and usual composure of Clarine was donned, and she straightened up and stepped closer to the door. Her fingers rapped on the metal. The sound reverberated through Keelin's body before it was engulfed by the Silence.

"Doctor Shaw, are you in there?"

"He's in here," Norton said coolly.

Clarine froze. She hadn't heard that voice since she helped admit him ten years ago.

In that moment, she had become more frightened than ever before: her heart beat quickened, her breathing became shallow, her eyes were unblinking, simply wide with fear. Keelin placed her right hand on Clarine's shoulder and took the keys from her pocket. She relaxed Clarine's hand with her touch and placed put the keys on her palm. When Keelin removed her contact, Clarine's hand began quivering again.

"It's Shaw, Doctor, you must help him, he's obviously in danger and this is your job."

Her whispers of encouragement seemed to work, and Clarine's fingers closed tightly on the metal in her palm. She found the key with the red plastic covering around the neck. She held it out and pushed it through the small hole. Excitement welled up in Keelin as she knew she was closer to being with Norton, which overshadowed every other feeling she had.

Excitement welled up inside me as I knew I was one step closer to Keelin. I hadn't seen her in only a few hours, but it seemed I had waited for her for days. As I heard the key turn in the lock, I positioned myself the way I had imagined the scene to play out. The door creaked open and light shone through the increasing gap. There was a woman I recalled from my first days here, but I hadn't known that she was Doctor Clarine. Beside her was my love, with a blue ribbon peeping out from behind her head and a small smile radiating from her gorgeous lips.

Clarine took a few steps in, the hand in her pocket clutching the syringe that contained a sedative. I smiled as I looked at her with an unblinking stare. She seemed to look slightly puzzled, then her face began to relax and the veins in her tense arms became less visible as she became almost at ease with the situation. She handed Keelin the keys, and Keelin silently locked the door behind them. She slipped off her shoes and left them by the door, without Clarine noticing. Keelin hadn't noticed the expression on Clarine's face, so her words were even more of a surprise to her ears.

"Oh my, you're—you're—*gorgeous*."

She stepped closer to me, her arms becoming increasingly outstretched towards me. I looked at Keelin but she did not look back—her glare was sending daggers towards Clarine, tearing at her horrid flesh. Adrenaline burst through Keelin and she lunged at Clarine. Clarine fell at my chest, her frightened eyes meeting mine before she was hurled away by her hair by Keelin. Keelin was slapping her face, tearing at her hair and kicking in every direction. Clarine was fighting back—her arms flailing as she reciprocated the blows she received.

"He's *mine*!" Keelin screamed through her grows and snarls. Keelin kicked Clarine back with her two legs. She jumped from the floor and the two women glared at each other from opposite sides of the room.

"What the hell has got in to you?" Clarine asked through gritted teeth.

"What the hell has got in to *you*?" Keelin spat back.

Their silent stare continued for another few minutes. Neither of them were speaking, simply staring, their bodies poised as if ready to pounce. Then, just as Keelin had done, I knew I would have to defend myself. Clarine's eyes met Shaw's limp body at the corner of the room, and suddenly all her anger became instantly directed at me. I was not afraid of her and I was planning to kill her anyway. She lunged at me. I

43

held out my hands to stop her but they did not touch her flesh. Keelin grabbed her and wrestled her to the ground.

"What have you done to him?" she screamed through her wailing.

"He's dead."

"*He's—dead?*" Clarine asked. Shock had quieted her voice to a whisper. She looked back at Keelin, as if wanting her to confirm my words. Keelin nodded and Clarine recoiled in fear. She crawled away from Keelin's grasp and stumbled over to Shaw's body. "No, please," she pleaded into his clothes as she buried her face in his chest. She looked back at us when she heard Keelin move. Keelin stood up and joined me by the window. Clarine's eyes fell on our joined hands and she stood up. Her frown vanished and an comprehending expression dawned on her face.

"You're going to kill me?" she asked, but Clarine knew it was rhetoric.

"I felt sorry for you when we were walking up here. I *actually* wanted to save you. Not anymore—the second you set eyes on him you're all over him! Who the *hell* do you think you are?"

"Oh shut up Keelin. He's handsome, I'll admit, I was just taken aback by his appearance. He was only a young boy when he arrived here. I guess I imagined him to be less, appealing, or whatever you want to call it."

She tried to remain focused on Keelin's face but her eyes kept diverting to mine with a flicker of desire burning through them.

"Well I'll have no trouble in letting him kill you *now*."

"How long has this been going on? What are you planning to do anyway? You're not going to get away with this—people will notice!"

"It's a recent thing, and we're planning to take over and escape. And no one will notice, because they'll all be dead," I replied, my mellow voice filling both the women's ears. They both looked at me, mesmerized by my deep tone.

"Take over *this* place? *No* one will listen to a pair of demented lunatics! You'll be *killed* before this day is out, I assure you."

"I was just about to say the same thing to you," Keelin said nonchalantly and she smiled with a wickedness I had not seen before. I looked at her and she looked at me. A dangerous streak flew through her eyes, and I had never been more attracted to her—a mesmerizingly beautiful killer who loved me and who wanted to be with me. What stroke of magic had brought her to me? I saw at the corner of my eye Clarine walking backwards towards the door. I looked up at her and then I saw it—the frightened look of shock that I had expected had arrived. She had decided to try to break free as best she could and she turned around and pulled the handle of the door. She pushed it down furiously with all her might, but to no use. She fell to her knees and the wailing began.

"Looking for these?" Keelin asked as she displayed the keys in the palm of her hand. Clarine's head turned.

"Give them to me, Keelin." Clarine said; her voice hoarse and whispered as she tried to regain what authority she had.

"No. I am with *him*, Clarine, and no one else means anything to me. I love him, and he is the one I'm going to fight for."

"You talk as if you're going into battle or something, Keelin. Give me the keys and come with me. His insanity is obviously influencing your judgment, because he can't love, he doesn't know how to. He killed his parents, he killed Shaw, the only one of us who listened to him, and he will kill *you*."

"No I won't, because I *do* love her. I'm fighting for her, for Silence and for ultimate happiness. You wouldn't understand, your mind is feeble like the rest."

"Help me!" Clarine was pounding on the metal door with her fists. We ran to her and I grabbed her waist and threw her back. Keelin jumped on top of her then and wrapped her hands around her throat. I remembered how this felt and went to kneel beside her. I had always respected Death, and no matter who died, a respect for their life was always necessary.

"Death is something we all must respect. Be glad that you have lived and embrace Death as something beautiful. Do not be afraid, there is nothing to be afraid of."

A final tear appeared at the corner of her eye as she looked up at me. The look of fear left her and a silent happiness glazed her eyes. As the tear meandered through her wrinkles that were painted on her complexion, I watched as it slowed and finally fell onto the hard floor that had ultimately been her death bed.

"Now you can release, Keelin; her final wish has been fulfilled and her soul has gone."

"You're so philosophical, Rupert," Keelin said with a smile as she looked at me.

"No I'm not; it's one of Nature's laws: A person's dying wish will be fulfilled and time will slow for the last earthly fragment to cease to be—it can be a tear, a final word or a final kiss. It can be anything that means a significant something to that person."

"How do you know Nature's laws?" Keelin asked with a ambiguity in her eyes.

"We are all part of Nature. If you completely surrender yourself to Nature and listen to the truth in your heart, you'll hear what she requires of you: her conditions, her truths and her rules."

When I finished speaking, reality washed back to Keelin and she suddenly realized what she had done. She looked into Clarine's dead and cold eyes. Sadness grew from her heart and penetrated her outer core as tears dripped from her motionless and icy eyes as she stared at her hands. I put my arms around her and hoisted her over to the corner where rays of light shone through the dust that hung at the bars of my window. I held her at my chest and cradled her. Her tears were full of words and emotions her body was not capable of expressing.

"I love you. Let the world heal your sorrow. Nature understands love; no matter what the price." I tilted her head towards the light and her skin sparkled with her heart's tears. "Sing to the forest, to the sea, to Nature." She looked at me and I kissed her salty lips. She opened her eyes again and began humming a tune I did not recognize. After a little while, she received the strength to muster words, and before long she was singing softly to the world beyond the walls that encased us. Her voice was like nothing I had heard. I was transported to a better place — a place where only Keelin and I lived; where the silent smile of Nature's rapturous song filled our ears. I listened to her tune and the words that flowed from her delicate lips.

She continued singing the Scottish folk tune and then her tone became strong and mellow. Outside, the birds in the trees nearby began singing with her, echoing with a harmony that balanced the beauty with a heavenly quality. A small songbird flew to the bars' edge, and positioned itself so it found the source of the singing. It sang with her until it looked to the sky as its family beckoned him. He flew off with a small flutter of wings and a small breeze met our faces as he took off.

"My mother used to sing that song to me when I was a child. I can't believe I *killed* Clarine, Rupert," she said and she looked at me, as if hoping for her sins to be cleansed.

"It should have been my death, not yours."

"How did you get past the sorrow?"

"The world rejected me. You know the origin of my power and strength. In my mind I am a beast, a cunning hunter of the darkness, of the midnight Silence. My mind is with Nature and not morality nor fairness; my mind is not like that of a human's, it is far more intelligent and quicker. Your mind and heart cannot deal with killing the way mine can. I am sorry. Love can make hearts and minds do strange, fascinating and dangerous things." I felt ashamed and guilty that I had not guarded Keelin from such heartbreak. I had thought she was like me, but I was wrong. I had been too premature in my assumptions. She looked at me again and put her delicate hand on my face. She looked into my eyes and looked so deep that I had the feeling she was reading my inner most secrets. I felt unfortified against her.

"I know you feel as if I am not like you at all, but I love you. This is not a simple passion, not a simple want; it's not even a blinding lust. It is love. It is a definite thing. Fate brought me to you—it brought us together. I may not feel exactly as you do, or cope with death the same way you do, but there is a definite bond between us. I love you and I am willing to be with you. We are together in this and that means that I am more like you than anyone else in this world." She looked at me with a love that poured from her eyes. Between us was an undeniable sense of unity, companionship and trust: love.

I put my hands on her face and kissed her. The kiss we shared was stronger, more passionate and more enthusing than anything that had gone before.. No one else mattered except her. No one else came close to making me feel the way she did. She was the one I loved more than myself; and I would give my life to help her, just as she had done for me.

Chapter Ten

Meanwhile, in central London, the Head of Psychiatry in the Central London Asylum, Doctor Conner Chambers, talked amongst his staff as to whom he was going to send to Scotland and help treat the infamous Robert/Rupert Norton. He was not surprised when there were minimal volunteers, but he *was* surprised to see three excited and waving hands reach up from behind the crowd.

"Who is that?" Chambers asked as he pointed to the three, still waving, hands.

"It's me, Doctor Chambers. Please may I go? I have been interested in his case since...forever. Please let me go and see him."

"Doctor Murphy, I have never seen you so enthused about your work in the time you have worked here. However, I cannot send you alone, he is a dangerous man—he's a serial killer. We can't take too many precautions."

The other two hands that had been beaten to the mark shot up again, and this time Chambers watched both hands sail above the crowd as their enthralled owners fought through their colleagues.

"Doctor Chase and Doctor O'Hare, I would like to ask you both a question. Why are three young men willing to travel to treat someone as strange as Norton?"

Doctor Chase stepped forward. His youthful blonde hair tossed in the light as he flung it from his face with a jerk of his head.

"Doctor, I studied Norton's case when I began work here, on my own time of course, and I have simply been waiting for an opportunity like this to arise. To my right, you see Doctor O'Hare, a highly intelligent man who simply can't survive without an exciting new prospect. And to your left you see Doctor Murphy, he has told you his reason for wanting to go, but if I was to tell you the truth, I would have to say that he simply cannot stand working here," he said with a smug smile at his now furious friend who stood opposite him. There was a murmur of anticipation as the staff waited for an outburst from the Chief of Psychiatry: it never came.

"Well, I think I am correct in believing that I will not get a more honest answer than that. Very well, you three may go; I was simply afraid that you might see this as more of a road trip than official work, that was all," Doctor Chamber said and he smiled at the three young men facing him. "Don't disappoint me lads, or you will not be getting a reference from this hospital, do you hear?"

"Yes Sir," they sounded in unison.

"Finish whatever assignments you have to finish. I will organise people to cover your shifts. You leave in two days. I expect you to be there by the third. Good afternoon staff. That will be all." The staff murmured a reply and dispersed, leaving three young men standing in silence in a deserting room, scared and pale faced as to what they had just signed up for.

Chapter Eleven

Keelin lay in my arms until the time came for her to return to her duty.

"What am I going to tell them when they start asking questions about Clarine and Shaw?"

"Tell them that you haven't seen them, and that everything is fine. They will be more concerned with me than with them anyway."

"What do you mean?"

"Did Shaw not tell you that because he couldn't treat me anymore, my personal dinners couldn't continue either? I'm going to be eating in the Cafeteria with the rest of the patients."

"No he didn't tell us that. Perhaps he left word on the notice board. I'll have to check it when I go down."

She got up, brushed the creases out of her cotton dress and redid the ribbon in her hair.

"Winter is approaching," I said. I could smell the cold breeze through the wind, and I knew the seasons were changing.

"It's only October, winter isn't due for another month at least."

"It's going to be a harsh one,." I said as I I looked to the sky and I could already see large, white and heavy clouds swim over the mountains beyond the forest.

"What are we going to do with these bodies Norton?"

I put my hands on her waist as I climbed to her height. When I was at my full height I looked down at her smiling face; she really was remarkably beautiful.

"Open the cell beside us and I'll help you move the bodies in now. In time people will have to get accustomed to the idea of walking me from here and back, it's best to do this when no one will venture here still," I said and she nodded.

"I'll come back when I'm ready."

She opened the door quietly and slid through the small ajar space. She looked back with a cunning smile before disappearing behind the closing door. I walked over to Shaw's body and hoisted him into my arms. His head and arms dangled from my forearms like a sleeping child's. I heard the metal door of the cell beside me click open and I heard her quiet, yet hurried, footsteps as they gathered back at my door. The door handle turned and her smiling face rejoined my presence.

"Everything is okay. Take him and I'll take her."

"Are you sure you can manage her?"

"I was strong enough to kill her so I think I'm strong enough to carry her," she said while she watched me leave the room with Shaw's lifeless body in my arms.

Keelin's eyes fell on her murdered victim. She felt sorry for what she had done, yet remorse did not fill her heart; there was almost a respect forming for Clarine. She hadn't known her very well; Clarine had made sure she kept her icy exterior ruthlessly cold and stern, making it almost impossible to have any kind of civil conversation with her.

She lifted Clarine's arms and put them over her right shoulder. Keelin had lifted dead weights before when dealing with her patients, but Carine's body was somehow heavier. Clarine was a slight woman and her auburn hair fell around Keelin's neck as she hoisted her up into her arms. She moved slowly out the door and walked into the cell to her left. Norton was standing beside Shaw's body, fixed in an upright sitting position.

"Right, I'm sure you'll see me soon for dinner."

When Keelin and Norton cleared everything that would attract attention, they kissed and parted. Norton went back to his lonely and empty cell and Keelin went back to her work. Neither of them could wait for dinner, apart from seeing each other again, they were both absolutely starving.

Chapter Twelve

Keelin's stomach sounded as she met the rest of her colleagues in the corridors. When she saw Paul walk towards her from the corridor, not only her stomach screamed—her inner voice screamed with fury. She couldn't stand the sight of Paul, his smarmy attitude filling the air around them with grease and dirt.

"Hungry?" Paul asked in his usual arrogant tone.

"My appetite only came back to me, I wasn't hungry before," she replied, questioning the idea of rambling on so she didn't have to hear his voice.

"I suppose that's understandable."

"Why would you say that?" Keelin asked, slowing her pace down as they walked down the corridor.

"Well, with your recent fear about Shaw and Norton, food would be the last thing on your mind."

"Oh right, yeah," she answered, moving along the corridor at a faster pace, hoping he wouldn't pry further into that incident, but she had no such luck.

"How did that turn out anyway?" he asked, and Keelin saw his face remain focused on her with interest.

"It was a false alarm; by the time we arrived there Shaw was outside Norton's room locking the door."

"He was in there the whole time?"

"I guess so."

"What about him not answering when you called again?"

"I never asked him about it; Clarine didn't give me the chance. She yelled at me for wasting her time and she marched back the way we came. Shaw simply smiled and walked off."

"Oh right," Paul said, nodding his head slightly. "Clarine didn't say anything to you regarding what we had been talking about earlier when you came in?"

"No. What *were* you saying about me anyway Paul? I never got the chance to ask you," Keelin asked. She had completely forgotten about it. She hated people complaining to Officials because of personal vendettas.

"Are you sure she didn't say anything to you?"

"I'm quite positive, Paul."

"I wasn't complaining about you, if that's what you think?"

"Oh weren't you, Paul? Because that's *exactly* what I think."

"I was talking to her about promoting you," he said. His voice was almost shy. Keelin stopped in her tracks and looked at Paul. His eyes moved from the ground to her gaze and then averted in a different direction.

"Why would you do that Paul?" she asked and she had a growing sensation of guilt for being so dismissive to him.

"You're a brilliant Nurse, Keelin, why else would she have listened to you earlier? She only gives her time to people she thinks have something important to say, and in her eyes, that excludes everyone but the important people."

"Thanks Paul. Look, I'm sorry I've been cruel and made things awkward between us. Sorry."

They began to walk again, and Keelin felt utterly ashamed of her recent behaviour towards him.

"Can I buy you coffee some time?"

"No. Look, Paul, I hope you didn't say those things to Clarine to try and be with me again?"

"Well I sort of hoped it would patch things up between us and you might take me back?"

"Paul, I'm sorry, but we ended because it was over. It's not as if either of us did anything to the other, our time just ran out, that's all."

"Do you think you could ever love me again?" Paul asked. He sounded desperate and pathetic, and Keelin felt sorry for him.

"Look Paul, I've met someone, and you have Angelina now anyway, and she's absolutely gorgeous; be happy with her."

"You've met someone?" Paul asked.

"Yes, Paul. We're over. Focus on Angelina now."

"Who the *hell* is he? You sleep and work here, so you can't have any time for anyone outside these walls. I know him, don't I?"

"Oh stop it, Paul. If you must know, you do know him."

"What?" Paul's fury screamed forth and he pinned Keelin to the wall.

"Get the hell off me, you idiot. Don't you *dare* touch me," Keelin said as she pushed against him with all her strength and he flew backwards, startling him with her strength. Keelin marched up to him and put her hand on his chest held him back against the wall. She was smaller than him, but his eyes shone with a frightened unknowing of what she was going to say. "Back...off! I'll say this once more Paul. Be happy with Angelina. Oh, and don't *dare* ask the staff questions about my personal life, or mark my words, it will be the last thing you do." She hit his chest with her clip board and marched through the corridor to the staff room just beyond. Paul remained still for a few moments and then ran after her, fury welling up inside him.

Keelin walked through the staff door and greeted everyone with her usual smile. She sat down with the rest of her colleagues and faced the white board that was assembled in front of them. Paul arrived a few minutes later with red eyes and remnants of water on his white coat and white cotton shirt. His eyes met everyone except Keelin.

An awkward silence spread through the Nurses and Doctors as their conversations decreased with the sight of Paul. The Nurses to the left of Keelin looked at her, but Keelin was staring at the white board; her focus on the small post-it with writing on it, stuck to its surface. Paul remained standing and took control of the meeting.

"Yesterday Doctor Shaw came to see me about Norton," he said and Keelin's heart raced at the sound of her lover's name. "He left me in charge of his case due to the fact that he has to cease treating him. I hope you will all give me your full support and obey any instruction I give you with regards to Norton." His gaze brushed over Keelin's and he rolled them in annoyance. It was clear he couldn't stand the sight of her anymore. "Shaw has given me instructions that Norton is to join the other patients for dinner in the Cafeteria." There was a murmur of shock before Paul spoke again. "This will commence from today onwards. I want everyone on board in this, understood?" There was a pause of shock before everyone nodded and another second passed before they verbally agreed. "Meet me here at five o'clock sharp. Make sure the other patients don't know what's happening; we don't want them starving to death. Oh and one final thing; Keelin Hogan had just announced that she has a new

man here, so could I have a round of applause for the doomed soul," he said with a smile so poisoned with anger that it hit Keelin like a shock wave. He applauded with loud, heavy and increasing claps, and the staff, while looking from Keelin to the male members of staff, clapped nervously and sporadically. Keelin could do nothing but stare at him. A small smirk etched its way onto her face; she would enjoy Norton tearing him apart. She would enjoy it immensely.

Chapter Thirteen

Five o'clock dawned and Keelin tried to swallow the excited feeling she had about seeing Norton. She didn't know whether the others would notice the wanting passion filling her expression when she saw him; she didn't know how she would react. She couldn't get over how childish Paul had been with the fact that she had found someone new. She should have expected it, though; he had acted in the same embarrassing manner when she had been going out with a Doctor from London. He had been studying Norton in a private assignment; Keelin had pulled a few strings and Shaw had allowed him to spend an hour with Norton, under Shaw's supervision of course. Keelin hadn't worked there a week and she had been bombarded with flowers and chocolates from Paul. When he saw Chase, he went crazy and had almost hit him. However, she grew to like him and when her job won over Chase, she began to date Paul, and they had been together up to four months ago.

The staff room filled with the twenty Nurses and Doctors that worked there. The other patients' dinner time had started at half four, so everyone was ready for Norton.

"I will only need ten Doctors, including myself to take Norton. The other ten go and wait in the Cafeteria and monitor the other patients. I want this to be as smooth as possible, okay? Any sign of Norton having one of his crazed notions, God forbid, we all use the sedatives provided, understood?" Everyone nodded, and Keelin saw the Nurses and Doctors either side of her wipe their sweaty palms on their uniforms. "Nurse Mary Cable, Nurse Angelina Ronston, Nurse Sarah Waters, Nurse Karen Black, Nurse July Hyde, Nurse Mary Becker, Nurse Rebecca O'Hare, Nurse Fiona Brown, Nurse Joy Fay, and Nurse Mable Carr, I would like you to go to the Cafeteria and follow the orders I have previously given you. The rest of you, that is, Doctor

Marlon Wright, Doctor Joseph Cape, Nurse Keelin Hogan, Doctor Thomas Dorian, Doctor Keith Matter, Doctor Justin Breda, Doctor Leonard Beau, Doctor Christopher McGrath, and Doctor Benjamin Cotton will be accompanying me to deal with Norton."

Silence answered his words. Angelina gave Keelin a sour look and shot Paul one too. She led the Nurses out of the door; attitude in each of their strides.

"Right let's go," Paul said, as he began to walk out the door.

As Keelin walked with her male colleagues, she burnt holes in Paul's back with her eyes. She knew exactly why he had put her in this particular group; it was for Paul to try and figure out who she was now dating. He kept looking at the men with suspicious eyes, and Keelin rolled hers every time, forcing back a scream by digging her nails into the palms of her hands

"You first, Doctor," Doctor Benjamin Cotton said, allowing Keelin to walk up the narrow staircase before him.

"Thank you, Benji," Keelin said, with a flirtatious voice, knowing Paul would overhear her affectionate term. She forced back a giggle as Paul eyed Benjamin and her from the top of the staircase. Benjamin's eyes caressed Keelin's behind as she curved her way up the stairs. When he arrived at the top of the staircase he met Paul. He grabbed Benjamin's collar and quietly spoke to him.

"Don't slip up with Norton, *Benji*...we wouldn't want you to get hurt."

Benjamin gave Paul a puzzled and bewildered look before being allowed to join the rest of his colleagues that had assembled before Paul and were awaiting further instruction.

Keelin's heartbeat began to quicken as her eyes looked down the corridor. A sensuous shiver ran through her spine and she wanted to run to Norton and jump into his strong arms. She managed to contain herself and focused on her hair blowing gently in the cold breeze that inhabited the corridor.

"Follow my instructions," Paul said and he proceeded to walk down the corridor that was draped in darkness, even though it was bright outside the stone walls.

The eyes of the men around Keelin looked at the dusty and dark walls; their frightened expressions deepening as they passed metal doors, knowing Norton's door was creeping upon them. Paul stopped short of Norton's door, and turned to them, but his eyes were fixed on Keelin and he addressed only her.

"I have read Shaw's case notes on this man, and it seems he had an unusual charm over women. I know you haven't a strong capability in controlling yourself when it comes to men, but if you could restrain yourself just this once, I think we'd all appreciate it." He grimaced at Keelin, and he laughed slightly along with the sniggers of the men beside her, and she had to say something.

"You're such a jerk," she said. "I hate you. I really do, and you wonder why I stopped loving you?" She stood and tried to stop her lip from quivering. "He's going to kill you...he's going to tear out your throat just for me...he's going to kill you for *me!*" She wanted nothing more than to scream those words, but she loved Norton too much to tarnish their plan and reconciled herself with the notion that she would make sure he killed Paul first. Paul turned away from them and he proceeded to walk down the corridor.

The key stopped short of the lock on Norton's door. Even through Paul's brave and pompous attitude before hand, he couldn't muster the strength to put the key in the lock and open it. He straightened up, his face pale and his hand quivering. His eyes fell on Benjamin, and his time to punish Keelin's new man had reared its head.

"Open this door Cotton," he said, standing back. Benjamin swallowed his fear and stepped forward. He took out his own set of keys and found the unused key with the red plastic coating on the neck. He bent slightly in front of the door and held out his quivering hand.

"Aren't you coming in?" Norton's voice appeared at the key hole and Benjamin flew backwards, landing, with the rest of the terrified men, against the wall opposite the door. Benjamin was midst silent tears when Keelin rolled her eyes and walked to the door.

"And you call yourselves brave, tough men?" She put her hand in her pocket and smiled at all of them as she found the red coated key. She turned away from them and then bent slightly, extending her hand.

"Keelin—," Paul said.

"I *will* open it, so you better be ready to do whatever you *strong* men intend to do. Or will I have to call up my ladies to do that too?"

The men regained their composure and walked slowly to the door. Keelin pushed the key into the lock and turned. The door opened slightly. The room was dark, except for a ray of light splitting the darkness on one side of the room.

A cool and collected young man stood at the barred and square shaped hole in the stone wall on the opposite side of the room. The artificial light in the corridor spilled through and illuminated him. He was leaning against the back wall, his arms folded, and a smile on his face. Keelin had never seen him more handsome; his white, cotton and torn shirt hung on his chest like an array of cloud; his long legs draped in black, torn and dusty trousers; his feet were bare, as usual, and his skin radiated against his long, black and untamed hair.

"Hello gentlemen, oh, and a lady," Norton said. His eyes moved slowly across Keelin's body; a delicious smile echoed on her lips, and then his eyes met theirs again. "Welcome to my humble abode. What can I do you for?" He opened his arms to welcome them, and smiled as he watched the frightened and aghast faces looking back at him, except for one…Keelin's. Keelin smiled devilishly as her eyes moved along his vigorous, exciting and striking body. He wanted nothing more than for Keelin to run into his arms and kiss him, and she wanted nothing more than to do so.

Chapter Fourteen

They put a strait jacket on him; they bolted him with chains attached to Doctors; they made sure that they treated him roughly; the made sure he was treated unfairly: slapped, punched and kicked before they began forcing him down the stone stairs. Keelin could do nothing but watch and try to act insensitively to the ordeal. If Shaw was there, he wouldn't have allowed them to have done that; but Shaw *wasn't* there, and that's why they did it. Norton dealt with the abuse with a wicked smile; he had been through far worse with his parents.

"Well, that's one way to work up my appetite. I'll make sure I finish the lot." He laughed and glanced at Keelin as they marched their way through the corridor, heading for the large room at the end of the corridor: the Cafeteria.

There were ten Nurses in the rectangular shaped glass office to the right of the entrance doors of the Cafeteria. The Nurses averted their gaze from their clip boards as Norton was pushed inside; shoved from behind by Paul and Marlon, the largest of the male Doctors.

"Oh...my..."

"Look at him."

"He's..."

"Absolutely..."

"Gorgeous."

"He's so...

"Dangerous. Look at those *eyes*..."

"Look, they're coming over here."

The Nurses instinctively fixed their hair and stood up, making themselves look presentable. They didn't exactly know what had come over them, but they looked nervously at one another, anticipating his arrival like schoolgirls. Giggles and squeals flew from their mouths as they watched him look up in their direction.

"We need to snap out of this. We can't let the men see us like this," Nurse Karen said. Although she was older than the rest of the girls, she couldn't help but fall for him too. There was something so dangerously alluring about him—it was indescribable, yet wonderful.

From the men's point of view, they saw ten frantic women just beyond them in the office, and presumed it was fear they felt. The men heard squeals muffled through the glass, and presumed they were cries of terror. However, Keelin recognized that they had just seen a gorgeous young man and he was walking their way.

Keelin smiled as she thought of how he had chosen *her*. She pondered on the thought that if some one else had gone to him, would he still have picked Keelin? She smiled as she knew *their* obsession was skin deep, and when they realized and remembered what a murdering man he really was, her competition would vanish. Besides, Keelin had killed some one already, and she had loved Norton from the second she had heard about him ten years ago; they were a part of each other now, she just had to contain her notions of killing the women who looked at him with wanting eyes like Clarine had done; Norton *was* the serial killer after all.

The Nurses in the office agreed to keep their notions from the men, and they tried to hide their bashful smiles as he spoke.

"Well hello ladies," Norton said as his eyes fell on the Nurses that greeted him in the glass room. Their eyes stared up at him and they assessed his strong and tall frame. His green eyes fell on them and they lost themselves in them, until his gaze was broken by Paul's hand slapping the back of Norton's head, sending it forward in pain.

"There'll be none of your so called verbal charm in here, understood?" Paul said into Norton's face and Norton glared silently back before speaking again.

"Oh I don't need any verbal charm, Doctor; I can bring a woman to me without saying anything at all."

"I'm surprised you know that, seen as you didn't *get* any women and I'm pretty sure you won't get a woman *now*."

"You'd be surprised who I can get, Doctor, perhaps even someone you thought would always be yours?" Norton asked. He smiled slyly at him and looked out through the glass window. Keelin felt nervous, and she could almost feel Paul's peripherals looking at her. "They look happy to see me, don't they?" The patients were all banging their cups and fists on the tables, screaming and crying like animals in the wake of a storm.

61

"You will go and get your food from the counter on the opposite side of the Cafeteria, and then you will sit where you wish and try to act like a normal and decent human being."

"You mean like yourself? I think I might be expecting that sedative if I acted like *you*. I'll act my own way. Oh, don't worry about me killing anyone, if I was going to kill some one, believe me, *you* would be the first to know."

"Is that a threat?" Paul asked.

"Call it what you will. Know that I am as unpredictable as the wind, and if you try to judge my actions then your arrogance might just come back and...bite you on the ass," Norton said and he laughed in Paul's face, his dangerous tone lifting with his final words. Keelin forced back a smile, as did the Nurses. Paul scowled into Norton's eyes and lifted the sedative from his pocket.

"Don't think I won't use it, Norton."

"Oh please do, I think *every*one is getting tired of your constant talk. You'll feel a slight prick but then you'll be *flying*."

Silence raged between them, and Paul grabbed Norton by the strait jacket. He pushed him to the door and made him face forward, towards the Cafeteria space.

"I'll kill you if I have to," he said in his ear before he unbuckled the chains and locks on his strait jacket. He pushed him forward so he fell down the steps on to the Cafeteria floor. He tore the jacket from him and smiled.

"Funnily enough, Doctor, I was just about to say the same thing to you."

I got to my feet as Paul closed the door and locked it. The patients around me settled slightly due to their fear; motionless and immobile because of it. I looked back through the glass that separated us, and I saw all their eyes on me, but I only returned Keelin's glare. I turned away and walked towards the metal serving counter on the opposite side of the Cafeteria. As I walked, a few eyes met mine before they quickly turned away in fear. I smiled to myself because I knew I could have a lot of fun with these patients; I loved the feeling I got from being feared.

Meanwhile, in the office, thoughts were swimming wildly in Angelina Ronston's head; she couldn't tear her eyes away from Norton. Her transfixed gaze was spotted by Keelin and Keelin knew that if Angelina wanted some one, she would pursue him until completely thrown back or accepted. Keelin looked at her reflection in the glass just beyond her face, and then her eyes moved to Angelina's. Her eyes moved over her perfect body; her beautiful blonde hair; her powerful and striking eyes embedded in a flawless face; her long legs that held up perfectly balanced curves. Keelin became worried that Norton's eyes would venture beyond her own body and rest on the body of a reckless flirt as she flaunted her assets.

Keelin's eyes moved back to Norton's body as he walked past scared and cowardly faces, and knew that she had to do something before Angelina did. However, to Keelin's dismay, she would soon learn that she hadn't acted soon enough.

Norton walked over and lifted the tray that had been left for him. The kitchen staff were in the far room of the kitchens, refusing to make contact with the killer. He turned around and the eyes in the room shot back to their dinners in front of them. Norton moved along the tables and saw an empty seat amongst a group of three men. He smirked and decided to torture them for a time.

"Good evening lads," I said as I put my tray on the wooden table with a loud thud. The rest of the room relaxed slightly as they realised I had found some where to sit—and it wasn't beside them. The eyes of the men sitting beside me were wide and their mouths had the same expression.

"It's *you*..." said the younger of the men who was sitting opposite me.

"It's me," I replied, extending my hand to shake his. He looked from my eyes to my hand and then nervously grasped it. "Rupert Norton, I'm sure you've heard of me." The man nodded and returned to his food; he kept his face low but his eyes watched me constantly.

"I thought—thought your name was Robert?" said the man to my right. He was older than some, but I suspected he was younger than the age his face told; his eyes were youthful like a child's, and it seemed he had the senseless curiosity of a child too. He had light brown hair, and is eyes matched it. The men stopped eating and looked at him with scared eyes, as if advising him to run.

"Well, I'm schizophrenic, y' see, so Robert would be my other half. We both thought it would suit our reputation if the blood thirsty serial killer represented us both...keep the air of danger, y' know?" I said my words in a nonchalant tone, and it produced mixed reactions.

"So you really *are* him?"

"Yes. I have seen you all a few times in my wanderings with Shaw, but I have only had a few of them, so am I right in presuming that most of you on this table only know me through rumours and whispers?"

"Some of us were here before you arrived, and some arrived after you, but, I suppose you are right, yes. I mean, you're so *young*. No one knew exactly what you looked like and any conversations that revolved around you were broken up immediately by the staff. Most of us had our own mind's picture of what you looked like, but, you're so different that I expected," said another man opposite me; he looked to be in his mid-thirties, and would have seemed completely sane, but I could tell by his fast speech, his constant blinking and the twitches he had in his hands, that, sadly, it was not the case.

"Well then, I'll just have to clear a few things up," I said and I pushed the tray to my left and kicked back my chair. I stood up on the table and cleared my throat. I could see the Doctors in the glass room run to the door, but I closed my eyes and held up my hand to them, and when I opened my eyes, they were watching me from the opposite side of the room—they had obeyed me, probably out of fear.

I looked into the glass room and saw the Nurses press their faces against the glass, trying to see me better. I watched as the kitchen staff ran along the wall and into the glass office: everyone was so afraid that I would cause trouble that the second I did anything; the protocol was to run and find a safe haven. I laughed slightly at the absurdity of them. I raised my arms and smiled, greeting everyone in my presence.

"Hello, my fellow mentalists, I would just like to formally introduce myself. I am Rupert Norton, but I prefer to be called Norton, so I advise you use that, alright? I hear most of you didn't know what I actually looked like, so I am here for all to see. I'm sure the friendly Doctors would organise a personal photograph of me if you asked politely. Oh, here they come. Well, enjoy your food, if you can call it that, and I hope to be seeing more of all of you," I said as I bowed and then jumped back to the floor. Paul was the first to reach me and he hit me at the back of the head again. I turned around and faced him. I was taller than him, but I could see a senseless anger in his eyes, and I wanted nothing more than to test it.

"Do you want me to sedate you? I said for you to do nothing, and you go and publically introduce yourself. Do you call that *nothing*?"

"I was just being courteous. Are you annoyed I didn't mention *your* name in there?"

"I hate being associated with you—you're a *freak*!"

"Oh, don't over react, Paul. You *love* being able to throw your weight around about me, I bet you're even thinking of starting a tourist business. I would think the autographs would sell quite well," I said as I smiled and jumped on the table behind him. He swivelled around. Because I was at an advantage and at a perfect position of attack, the rest of the Doctors retreated a few steps, but Paul refused to. I smiled as I walked along the table, the patients moving their trays towards them to let me walk past.

"Everyone else might be afraid of you, but I am not," Paul said as he followed me.

"Is *that* why you couldn't turn the key earlier?"

"How did you know that was me? Besides, I was expecting someone a little more frightening. I mean, *look* at you—you're nothing but a young, pathetic man who everyone hates."

"Hates me? I think you'd be surprised if I told you who *loved* me." I said with a smile as I jumped off the end of the table and walked briskly towards the angry man standing like a raging bull. I walked straight up to him; he wasn't moving and I loved a challenge. I stopped so close to him that our faces nearly touched. I leant forward so that my lips were at his ear. I could feel the bristles of his hair collide with my shaggy black mane; I could feel the shiver it caused as it spiralled through Paul. "As for being frightened, when the time comes for you to feel *real* fear, when it pulses through your mind, and nothing else exits, you'll meet me. Soon, *Doctor*," I said as I brushed my shoulder with his and returned to my seat, taking a great bite out of the bread roll on my tray.

Paul was left standing, immobile with terror, in the place Norton had left him; his chest tight with a growing feeling of insecurity and helplessness. He forgot where he was, and when his conscious mind alerted him, he turned without another glance at
Norton, and walked out of the Cafeteria, pale faced and red eyed. The staff exchanged bewildered glances, and then retreated to the glass office and waited for Norton to finish his food before they began bringing him back to his cell.

A satisfaction welled up in Keelin's chest and she couldn't help but smile. She was so proud of Norton. She couldn't stop smiling, and she was oblivious to Angelina beside her. Angelina had followed the direction of her gaze and looked from Keelin to Norton. Angelina tossed her long hair with her hands, straightened her pinafore at her bust, and smiled with determination as she walked towards the door. She turned back just before closing the door, and spoke calmly.

"I'm going out to him," she said and they all looked at her with shocked expressions.

"No, you can't handle him," Doctor Marlon said as he stepped towards her. She stopped him with her hand.

"Oh don't worry about me, I can handle *any* man," she said and her sensuous voice filled the men's ears and her eyes met with Keelin's momentarily before her long hair disappeared beyond the door. Keelin's heart sank, and she had to restrain her legs from running out the door after her.

Chapter Fifteen

Paul's head pulsated with frustration and his walk developed into a run as he headed for the staff room. He burst through the door, and the second he had done so, tears flew from his eyes, and he fell to his knees. He felt many emotions; he felt terrified of Norton, angry that he had let him get to him, and completely vulnerable, so much so that his heart and soul needed to release his pain to help him, and somehow, comfort him. He got to his feet and lifted one of the chairs in front of him. He threw it at the wall to his left. He watched it as it bounced off and landed in the corner. With a scream, he dug his fingers into his head as the tears streamed from his eyes.

Meanwhile, Angelina meandered past the tables in the Cafeteria, moving towards Norton who sat at one of the far tables. The heads of the men turned in her direction as she walked confidently past them. Her black kitten heels sounded on the floor with each step she took. She didn't wear any jewellery because it was forbidden, but she had her blood red lipstick that she religiously wore. Her long hair tossed behind her as she steadily walked. Norton didn't notice her until the last second. He looked up as she turned the corner of the table and neared him.

"That's a sight for sore eyes," said the man opposite Norton.

There was no one sitting to Norton's left, so Angelina took full advantage of that. She kicked the chair away with her heel, and slid onto the table, angled towards Norton, her legs crossed, her nails rapping on Norton's tray. She waited for him to look up at her face before she stopped, and then she spoke. She held out her hand to Norton.

"I'm Nurse Angelina Ronston. It's a pleasure to make your acquaintance." Norton shook her hand and nodded, and sat back in his chair, assessing her face. She knew he was watching her eyes, so she slid her gaze over his body, and one of her eyebrows rose as she met his face again. "You're a very handsome man," she said, smiling.

"You'd be surprised how much I've received that recently."

"I don't think it *would* surprise me," she said and a delicious smile broke the sea of red that was her lips.

"What can I do for you?" Norton asked, looking into her eyes.

"Oh, I'm sure you could do a lot of things for me, Norton," she said, hardly breaking her smile to speak. She moved slightly closer to him, assessing his legs. She wanted for him to grab her and sit her on his lap and kiss her red lips—

"I'm not interested," Norton said, folding his arms. Her eyes darted up to his and she laughed slightly.

"Not interested in what?"

"I'm not interested in *you*."

"Good. Keelin wouldn't be too happy. I think she sees me as a threat. I can't say I blame her," she said and relished in Norton's eyes as their pupils widened at her words.

"I don't know what you are talking about."

"Well, let's presume that you do, for time's sake," she said as she looked at the clock on the wall. "I want to ask you something."

"Ask away, Nurse."

"Do you really think *she's* prettier than I am?" she asked. Angelina's face was stern and cold now and not even a menacing smile broke her complexion.

"Yes. Keelin has something that you, simply…lack," Norton said, and the man beside him choked slightly on his food. He coughed and looked at them apologetically.

"I'll keep your secret quiet. I want some excitement as much as the next guy. *Really*, Norton, do you think she is attr—?"

"Yes. There is no denying that you *are* beautiful, but you're not Keelin, so you're not attractive to me," Norton said and he smiled as he thought of Keelin.

"Well, that's all. I suppose I'll see you around, Norton."

She walked away with a cunning and devilish smile starting on her face.

"You'll keep quiet about what you just heard, won't you lads?" I asked around me. They nodded and I could almost hear words resting on their lips as they stared at me. "You can ask what questions you want, but we have to stick together, okay? I don't know your names, so say your name before you ask me something." They nodded briskly, and the man to the right of me spoke first. He had ginger hair and his eyes were a bright blue.

"I'm Kevin. Were you talking about Nurse Keelin?"

"Yes, Kevin. Nurse Keelin and I are…involved with each other." Amazed eyes followed my words. "If I hear about any of this from any one other than you three, then I will come to you in the night and kill you all, understood?"

They swallowed in fear and nodded.

"Keelin is the only member of staff who is kind and nice to us. The rest never let us *be*. They are so cruel with their words, especially Paul," Kevin said, and he pushed his food away, as if the thought of Paul made him lose his appetite.

Keelin's eyes followed Angelina as she walked out the Cafeteria door, the eyes of the men still following her figure. Keelin was beginning to get worried about what she and Norton had talked about, but she had the nervous suspicion that it would not benefit their situation one bit. She had never trusted Angelina and her instincts about people's characters had never failed her, and she wasn't about to start doubting herself now. She bit her lip and focused on the clip board in her hand, trying to act as normal as possible.

Chapter Sixteen

Paul was looking in the mirror on the wall of the staff room. The door opened and he saw Angelina walk over to him. He turned around and felt Angelina's hands push him back against the wall. She was slightly smaller than him, but she stood on her toes and kissed him. Her red lips looked like blood against snow in comparison to Paul's. He wrapped his arms around her thin waist and lifted her to his height. He moved her over to the kitchenette and her back met the fridge. He ran his fingers through her flowing hair and pressed her body against the fridge with his. Through kisses Angelina spoke.

"I have—some very—important—information—for you, Paul—"

"It can wait," he said.

"It's about Norton, and Keelin," she said and she felt his lips leave hers as he looked at her. Her red lipstick had smudged on his lips, and his eyes were still red

The sexual tension mounted in the air as Keelin and her colleagues brought Norton back to his cell. Norton walked in front of Keelin up the spiral staircase. She couldn't help but want to touch him. There was no one behind her, so she didn't see any harm in tapping his behind slightly as he climbed the stairs. She smiled and restrained a giggle. He felt her hand press against him. He tried to restrain a grin as he thought of her cheeky smile. They couldn't wait to be alone again; they missed the satisfaction a kiss could bring.

Angelina told Paul everything Norton had said. He kissed her again, proud of her cunning mind. As she reapplied her lipstick and combed her hair, she straightened her uniform and stood up from the couch.

"If we play their game, and play ours better, we'll be able to get her locked up too," she said. He smiled with a devilish grin, and Paul's fury for both of them overwhelmed him, and he nodded, grabbing her waist again and dragging her back onto the couch; their menace and conniving sealed with vowing kisses of secrecy, vengeance and jealousy.

Seven o'clock dawned and Norton was back in his cell and being locked in for the night. Keelin and Norton exchanged a lingering stare as she closed the door to his cell. She heard the clicks of the lock and put her keys back in her pocket. Some of the Nurses had come with her to lock him up; the Doctors had dispersed due to the fact that Paul wasn't there to give orders, and they wouldn't go near Norton unless forced to. Nurse July bit her lip and spoke with a smile.

"Keelin, we've decided this is just a girl thing, the men aren't to know, or they'll think we're crazy. I know we shouldn't think it, but isn't Norton *gorgeous*?"

Keelin stopped dead in her tracks, and looked at them.

"Come on Keelin, you have to admit, there's something about him, something *dangerously* attractive," Nurse Rebecca O'Hare said, supporting July.

"I suppose so, kind of," Keelin said, resisting the urge to answer with "of course he's *gorgeous*! Look at him, but back off he's *mine*." They descended the narrow staircase and Keelin thought of how many hours would pass before she could secretly

ascend them again to meet with her love in the darkness that draped and hid them in the night.

71

Chapter Seventeen

"I'll work the night shift tonight, so I can sleep tomorrow, is that okay with everyone?" Keelin asked her colleagues as they assembled back in the staff room, either to clock on or off. The staff agreed; none of them really cared either way. She took a final look at who she was working with tonight: Nurse Sarah Waters, Nurse Marie Becker, Nurse Fiona Brown, Doctor Christopher McGrath and Doctor Joseph Cape. She agreed that she wouldn't have a lot of trouble in sneaking off to see Norton; everyone normally stayed in the staff room unless they were called or something happened. As the people who weren't on rota started to walk towards their separate sleeping chambers, (converted cells on the bottom floor) Keelin and the rest of her colleagues who were on call began the ritual of making sure all the patients were in their cells and the cells were locked securely. Keelin, Marie and Sarah walked the short flight of stairs to the second floor and they began their night shift.

"That's it, Clive, in to your room," Keelin said as she directed a lone patient standing in the corridor. He shuffled in to his room and Keelin locked the door after him.

When all the patients had been accounted for and the doors were double-checked, they began to retire with heavy heads to the staff room. Keelin thought it would be wise to accompany them so it didn't seem suspicious. Keelin ran and jumped onto the couch, and when she heard a loud crunch she jumped up. She lifted a large toiletry bag full of make-up.

"Angelina left her make-up here," she said, throwing it on the coffee table before her. Her eyes kept drifting back to the make-up in front of her, and an idea presented itself to her. "I'm going to take a shower, okay?" she said, standing up and walking through to the back room where the lockers were situated. She walked to the mirror that hung on the wall and mused. *If I'm going to be with a dangerous killer,*

I think he should have a girl who looks dangerous too. She looked at her flawless complexion and thought of it like a blank canvass. She thought of Angelina's ability to look great, and she decided to show her how gorgeous *she* could be. The ribbon was now holding in place hair that was frizzed and messy. As she took the ribbon out of her hair, she shook her head, and walked to the shower room beyond.

When Keelin returned to the mirror she was refreshed, renewed and ready to revitalize her body. She hadn't taken care of her appearance in so long, but tonight was going to be a good night, she could feel it. She opened her locker and reached past her recent things and felt for her old uniform. With a smile she shook the creases out of the cotton and laid it out on the bench beside her. She threw away the things perched at the front of her locker and brought her make-up, blow drying brushes and old beauty products back from the dead.

She rubbed moisturiser all over her skin and watched the droplets of water be absorbed alongside the moisturiser. She repositioned the towel around her body before laying out two blow-drying brushes, her comb and her large brush, used to straighten her hair even more so. She grabbed the hairdryer and began working on her hair.

When her hair was fully perfected, it radiated and shone with a silky shine she had forgotten how much she loved. She donned her underwear and then slipped on her old uniform. The uniform was smaller than her baggy one that she wore regularly. She smiled at her reflection; she had forgotten what her body looked like in a dress that hugged at her hips and curved past her bust and bum. She had grown slightly and so her dress was just above her knees, but she felt proud of herself in it, and for the first time in a long while, she felt gorgeous.

She reacquainted herself with her make-up, lining her eyes with a strong black, pumped up her eyelashes with her volume enhancing mascara and ran her lipstick over her plump lips, staining them with a rich, seducing and blossoming pink. She twirled in the mirror and looked at her hair; she used to be so proud of it, and she had let her maintenance diminish and it had resulted in lifeless, bland and boring hair that's only excitement was a ribbon every so often. But now, her fringe, which she had almost forgotten existed, framed her face in a side parting, and her feathered hair kissed the sides of her face as it draped past; the layers in her hair fell along her back until it rounded off delicately at her base. She had forgotten how long her hair had grown. It bounced as she walked towards the mirror and looked at herself from different angles. She excitedly threw her things back into her locker and took a deep breath, ready to present her new self to her colleagues.

She strode confidently from the back room through to the staff room. Joseph was at the kitchenette. His eyes scanned Keelin's body as she smiled at him. She struck a pose when she reached the sleeping people in the couch. Christopher's eyes opened slightly but then shot open when he saw her. Christopher blinked and woke the female Nurses who were asleep beside him. They beamed when they saw her.

"Damn girl, you are *hot*," Marie said.

"Why did you get dolled up?" Rebecca asked, standing up and assessing her from different angles. Keelin smiled and shrugged her shoulders.

"I guess I just have a good feeling about tonight."

"So it's true you have a new man? Paul was so mad," she said with a laugh

"Yes, I do have a new man."

"Who is the lucky lad?" Christopher asked. "Is it Benjamin?"

"No. You do know him, but I'm not telling you who he is," she said with a smile at their begrudged faces.

"Why are you getting dressed up at night?" Marie asked, and then she gasped and looked at Joseph. "*You* haven't said much. Are *you* the new man? That's why she's getting dolled up, he's on call *tonight*."

"I wish," Joseph said.

"He's not on call. I'm actually going to his room now, so I'll see you later," Keelin said as she put her index finger to her lips and then gave them a cheeky smile before she walked out the door. Keelin smiled and shook her head as she turned a corner in secrecy and headed quietly in the direction of the top floor.

She crept up the stone stairs like a sprite and ran lightly down the corridor that was lit dimly by artificial light. She delicately and slowly turned the key in Norton's cell door, trying to make as little noise as possible. After pulling the key back out and putting it back in her pocket, she took a final glance down the corridor. Then she turned the handle and proceeded to open it.

The moon was exceptionally strong through the window and my whole cell was lit with a silver glow. I heard Keelin draw near and excitement grew from within me. I stood up and waited for her at the opposite side of the room; I had a great feeling about tonight. The door opened and I saw her. She was the sexiest thing I had ever seen. Her hair bounced around her as she swung around the door; her body was

74

enhanced by her tight dress and her legs were elongated with its shorter length. Her eyes and lips were accentuated by her make-up and I couldn't seem to believe such a beautiful woman was in the same room with me, never mind that she wanted me as much as I wanted her.

She looked like Aphrodite herself as she clung to the door, as if restraining herself from losing control. But she couldn't fight me any longer. She kicked her shoes off and paused before running to me. With a leap in the air, she landed around me; her lips met mine before I knew what was happening; her legs wrapped themselves around my waist and her arms wrapped themselves around my neck. The force of her impact pushed me back against the wall and I put my arms around her body, supporting her. My hands ran over her body as if she would disappear and I needed to memorize every part of her. She looked at me and whispered with a passion that burned at her tongue.

"I've never loved some one as much as I love you. I want to be a part of you." She kissed me again, and then I replied.

"You have me. I'm all yours. I am a part of you, I always have been and I always will be," I said as I slid my back down the wall. She fell back onto the ground and as I kissed her, the darkness consumed our bodies.

Chapter Eighteen

Keelin awoke in Norton's arms to the sound of footsteps beyond the cell door. She shook Norton as she sat bolt upright. Norton put his index finger to his lips and motioned for her to remain silent and to move into the corner. Norton silently got to his feet and walked to the door. He closed his eyes and smelt the air; he then knew who was outside the door. He stepped closer to the iron slide, his eyes directed forward. The slide opened and Keelin heard a man scream and jump back.

"Hello Paul," Norton said. Keelin's eyes widened with fear. What would she do if he demanded to come in?

"I should come in there and kick the hell out of you."

"Oh, be my guest Paul, I'd love to fight you, but are you sure this corridor is the best place to fight with me, though? I mean, no one would hear you scream for help," Norton said with a smug smile.

"I'll have you, Norton," he said and his voice was whispered and Keelin knew he was flat against the door. Their eyes were inches from each others'. Keelin didn't know why, but she suddenly got a rush of excitement, and she couldn't help herself. She began to crawl towards Norton. The iron slide was still open and both men were staring at each other.

Keelin met his ankles. She crouched behind him. She began to slowly run her hands up the back of his legs. Her fingers walked their way over his cotton black trousers. Her hands met his ass and her hands felt him as they curved to the base of his back. Norton stared at Paul with a grin. Paul eyed him suspiciously. Her arms were outstretched above her as her hands followed his long back. Her legs began to straighten as she neared his shoulders. Just as Keelin's fingers wrapped themselves around his shoulders, Paul closed the iron slide and walked off. Keelin straightened completely, and turned Norton around to face her. He smiled as he shook his head.

"You couldn't just remain in the corner, could you?"

"No, Norton, you know me. I wanted my fun too," she said with a pout. He bit his lip and grabbed her, kissing her.

"You want fun?"

"I want fun," she said with a nod. Norton smiled and then thumped his fist on the door behind him. "Paul," he shouted. Keelin's eyes widened as she looked at him. Footsteps gathered around his door again and just as the iron slide opened again, Keelin crouched at the wall beside the door.

"What?"

"Have you seen that really gorgeous Nurse?"

"Are you talking about Angelina?"

"No, not her."

"There are no other gorgeous Nurses."

"Oh, is Keelin Hogan a Doctor?"

"Why are you asking about her?"

"I was just asking if you have seen her body lately. She is *nice*," Norton said and he grinned into Paul's face as he became angrier.

"Shut up," Paul said through gritted teeth.

"Why isn't a fine young Doctor like you with her? Oh, you *were* with her weren't you? She always loved some one else, though, didn't she?"

"How do you know about her personal life?" Paul asked, closing the distance between Norton's face ands his.

"I pick up on things, Doctor. I hear things, conversations in the night."

"You're such a freak," Paul said and his eyes scanned the room and then looked suspiciously back at Norton. "I haven't seen Keelin this morning, Norton. She wouldn't be in there with you would she?"

"I wish," Norton replied, with a curve of his lips.

"I'll be watching you, Norton."

"That's good to know," Norton said and he could see fear flicker in Paul's eyes, and he knew that he wouldn't enter. Norton smiled and retreated back into the room. Paul watched him and then rolled his eyes and shut the iron slide, walking back through the corridor.

Keelin took the longer route back to the staff room. Her hair was still full of volume, and her appearance was still as exciting as the night before. She walked confidently through the corridors and ran to her room. She waited there for a while, then freshened herself, gathered her work things and walked to the staff room. She wanted to change out of her smaller uniform; her looser uniform was more practical. She hadn't realized what the time was until she checked her watch in her locker. It was half four by the time she returned to the staff room. Keelin heard the people who were on call leave the staff room to bring the patients to dinner. Keelin jumped in the air when she turned and saw Paul leaning against the lockers on the opposite side of the room. He was watching her. She scowled at him and then took her loose uniform out of the locker.

"Do you mind?" she said, holding up her uniform and indicating the door.

"I don't mind at all," Paul said, but he didn't budge and he remained staring at her. She rolled her eyes and turned away from him. She pulled her dress off and quickly threw the other one on. *Paul, you're such a perverted creep.* She turned around and looked at him and folded her arms.

"What the hell is your problem?" Keelin asked as she fired her other uniform into her locker.

"Where were you this morning?" Paul asked.

"I was in my room," she said and looked at him with hatred in her eyes, and he reciprocated.

"No you weren't."

"How do *you* know?"

"You weren't there. Don't deny it."

"I'm not denying it. You seem pretty sure of yourself, Paul."

"I *know* you weren't there," he said. Keelin opened her mouth in shock as she realized why he was so certain.

"You *didn't* come into my room, did you Paul?" Paul remained silent. She grabbed her clip board, gathered her things and began to walk out of the locker room. She stopped and pointed her finger at Paul's face. "This has got to stop, Paul. I thought you had given me back the spare key to my room after we stopped dating, but you know what, keep it, I'd rather get my locks changed." She scowled at him. She began to walk away when he grabbed her arm and threw her back into the lockers. He lowered his face to hers and locked her in that position with his hands.

"I know where you were."

"Where was I? Why the hell should you care anyway Paul? It's starting to get creepy," she said and she tried to move away from him but he was too strong.

"I know you've always had this weird fantasy about Norton. I know you're involved with him, or want to be. I'm taking you off his case. You're getting too close."

"Close...I've never spoken to him, you idiot."

"Don't insult my intelligence, you stupid little brat."

"What the hell have you been taking? You're crazy."

"If I see you any where near him, or having anything to do with him, or...not doing your job I'll go straight to Shaw or Clarine!"

"Go to them now. I want you to tell them your paranoid ideas, and see what they say when you present no evidence."

"Don't test me, Keelin."

"You think you're so amazing, don't you? Grow up and shake the jealousy from your self. I'm involved with some one, yes, but it's not *Norton*. I told the people who I was working with last night where I was going, and I don't believe you were on duty last night."

"Look, watch yourself, or I'll expose you, and Norton."

"*Goodness sake. You're* the psycho. You're such a demented creep. I'll report you for being mentally unstable if you do not leave me alone. I'll report you for sexual harassment too if you keep stalking me." She tore his arms away from hers, wacked him with her clipboard and them stormed from the room.

Angelina met Paul outside the staff room. She had seen Keelin leave and had waited for Paul, just as they had agreed.

"Well?" she asked as they began to walk.

"She denied the whole thing. We're going to have to keep away from Norton, though, she'll tell him, and we don't know what he might do to stop their secret being heard," Paul said and they walked off through adjacent corridors, a mixture of fear and excitement soaring through them.

Chapter Nineteen

Keelin's heart was beating faster than it had ever done. She felt tears well up in her eyes, and she broke into a run but she didn't know where she was running to. She wanted to run to Norton's cell but she knew she couldn't after what Paul had said. Tears poured from her eyes as she ran into the grounds. The cold air hit her face and slowed her feet. She dropped to the grass and buried her face in her hands. Her body heaved as she cried. She gripped the earth in her hands and remembered what Norton had told her. *Nothing but Nature understands me.* She knew exactly what he meant now. She lay down on the grass and felt the world around her comfort her. She felt as if everyone in her life was a threat to her and she felt the weight of society's expectations on her body. She never realized how much she hated society's rules. She wanted everyone just to let her *be. Why can't people simply let me be?* Pressure built up inside her and she wailed.

"Why can't you all just let me be...just let me live."

I heard Keelin's voice from beyond my cell. I heard her cries and I knew something had happened. Paul was behind her pain, I was sure of it, and so I formed a secret plan in my mind. As dinner time approached, I made a promise to Keelin that Paul would die tonight. I closed my eyes and tried to calm her. I had experienced the power of my mind before; because my mind was completely open and all sections of my mind was charged and being used. I was able to control things with my mind. In the very deepest corner of the mind, insanity lurks, and it is through this I find freedom. My mind tortured me at times, but I learnt to deal with it and the Silence helped; I only needed myself and the Silence in the world. All aspects of my mind were let loose; including the magic.

Keelin felt an overwhelming sense of calm. Her body felt as if Norton was holding and comforting her and she knew Norton had heard her. She smiled as she saw Norton in her mind's eye and she listened to his words. Gaining the strength to stand up, she brushed the dirt from her clothes, and wiped the tears from her eyes. She took a deep breath, walked through the door and walked to the Cafeteria; smiling because she knew Paul would die tonight.

Chapter Twenty

Norton was escorted through the corridor towards the Cafeteria. He looked amongst the faces of the Doctors and Nurses that walked beside him and he didn't see Paul; he hoped he would be in the office in the Cafeteria because he could hardly wait to silence his disgusting and ugly voice. Norton felt a vengeance creep up from within him as he saw Paul's recoiling face in the glass office of the Cafeteria.

They untied the strait jacket and left me to rip it from my body; enough time for them to get inside the protective glass office. I threw the white and heavy jacket to the ground before I walked over to the lonely metal kitchen and lifted my tray that had been abandoned on the ledge. I walked over to the three men I had been sitting beside yesterday. They looked up at me as I approached, and they donned a nervous disposition. I smiled and sat down beside Kevin.

"Hello lads, don't look so nervous, it's only me after all." I tore at my bread roll with my teeth and eyed Paul's pompous movements in the office ahead of me. I knew my time to bring Paul to me had arrived. I finished my food and then smiled to the men beside me. "Have you ever seen someone being murdered?" I asked with a dangerous smile on my face. They glanced nervously at each other and then shook their heads silently. "Then this is your lucky day," I said and I kicked back the chair and stepped on to the table. I raised my hands and moved my fingers; indicating for Paul to come to me. The staff in the glass office exchanged nervous glances with each other and then their eyes fixed on Paul. Paul slammed his clip board on the desk and stormed out of the office.

I watched his strides bring him closer to me and when he reached the table I was standing on I jumped down and we squared up to each

82

other. His chest was pushed out; his macho persona screaming forth. I smiled with a deathly vengeance.

"What the hell do you want now?" Paul said, and his fingers groped for the sedative in his pocket.

"Are you ready to feel the fear of death?" I whispered, hardly opening my lips. The audience of patients were staring at us; they knew something was going to happen because this was the second time Paul and I had been here. Paul laughed slightly and then rolled his eyes.

"You're not going to kill me," he said and one of his eyebrows rose.

"It'd be the highlight of my week," I said as I smiled into his eyes and I saw adrenaline soar through him.

"Go for it."

"Don't you want to hear my reasoning?"

"I suppose," he said as he went to sit down on the chair.

"I wouldn't make yourself too comfortable, you won't be here for much longer."

"You make a lot of empty threats, Norton." Paul folded his arms and sat back in the chair. His confidence had definitely grown since the last time they had talked.

"I'm going to kill you because of Keelin, and the abuse you've given her over the past while."

"She's not so willing to tell the truth as you are; she must be ashamed of you. I don't blame her—" Paul didn't have time to finish his insult. His words had struck a nerve and I threw my fist into his face. I kicked his chest and he stumbled backward. He scrambled amongst the chairs to stand up. I stepped forward with my fists clenched and threw my fist into his face three times. He stumbled back and then fell onto the floor. I jumped on top of him and put my hands around his neck. His face began to throb due to the stopped blood flow. His fingers clawed at mine and then I felt him fighting back. He threw his fist into the base of my back. He continued to lay his fists in to my spine and my strength buckled. I loosened my grip and punched him once more before standing up again. He rubbed his neck in shock and looked around for his staff; they were immobile in the office, staring blankly at the scene that was unfolding before them. He resorted to the sedative and took it out of his pocket as he leant on the chair and stood up. His shocked face met mine and I smiled. To my surprise, he smiled back.

"You didn't expect me to fight back, did you?"

"Actually, I'm glad you did; it'll make my victory that much sweeter."

I began walking towards him and he did the same. We strode towards each other. He lunged at me with the syringe. I turned, dodged it and grabbed his wrist, turned it and felt it break within my grasp. Pain shot through Paul's face and then it erupted from his mouth. At that, I heard screams from afar and I saw the staff try to run to his aid, but there was someone stopping them: Keelin.

She was punching the colleagues as they tried to get past her. Paul's other hand smacked against my face and I stumbled back. I kicked the sedative across the floor and I threw my knee into his stomach. After winding him, he fell to the floor. I forced my knee into his nose again and pinned him to the ground. I wrapped my fingers around his neck again and stopped the air entering his body once more. Tears spilled from his eyes as he glared up at me. I raged with anger I had only felt when I had killed my parents. He had insulted Keelin's love for me and it had set my vengeance into overdrive.

Death came to Paul swiftly and I honoured it once more. I told him not to be afraid and to embrace the peace that he was becoming enveloped in. When he finally died I sat up and shuffled away from him. The patients obviously hated Paul and applause began to echo around the Cafeteria. I heard a thundering sound and I looked up to see Keelin running after Angelina and the rest of her staff as they hurtled towards me; she hadn't been able to hold them any longer.

I didn't want to do anything but as Angelina ran towards me she began screaming; it was a piercing scream and it hurt the Silence that death had created. She hurtled towards me, and when she reached me I grabbed her neck quickly and jerked it to the side. She fell like a rag doll, limp and lifeless. She was dead. I had broken her neck and the sound had stopped the others in their tracks, except for Keelin. Keelin jumped over the bodies strewn on the floor and jumped into my arms, kissing me with her passionate lips.

"I'm so happy you did it. He was *torturing* me. Oh, I love you so *damn* much." She yelled as she held me closer. I kissed her back, both of us forgetting where we were. I twirled her to the sound of applause, and then a muffled sound drenched my ears, and Keelin slipped from my arms.

I had felt a tiny prick on my neck and then I began to fall. My knees buckled and I collapsed on the ground. Keelin was sedated after me and I felt her head against my chest as my mind drifted away; the only sound in my mind was the applause and Robert's approval of what we had done; we were merging into one, and it felt just as it had done when I was first awoken.

Nurse Marie had run down an isle between the tables and had approached Norton and Keelin from behind, while the rest looked on from the opposite side with scared and shocked faces. While Keelin and Norton lost themselves in each other she had struck his neck with the sedative she had taken from her pocket, and struck Keelin with the sedative she had retrieved from the floor, which had been Paul's.

Chapter Twenty-One

Meanwhile, in London, Doctors O'Hare and Murphy were waiting for Chase in the foyer of the hospital; their suitcases packed and ready for the trip. Chase had drawn the short straw and he would be driving them to Scotland...in his black Ferrari.

The sound of the engine sent shivers through the Doctors' bodies as they saw Chase drive to the front doors and stop. Chase beckoned with his hand for them to get moving. They walked towards the car and paused at its metal; afraid of touching the beautiful machine that sat before them. Chase pressed a button inside the car and there was a click as the doors unlocked.

"Get in," Chase said through the opening window. Murphy locked his fingers around the metal handle and sat in the customized black leather seat that hugged his body. O'Hare sat in the back; they didn't realize they had left their suitcases on the pavement. Chase shook his head and shoved Murphy out of the car.

When the boot was loaded with their three suitcases, Chase revved the power that he controlled and turned the car around. The sound of the tires against the gravel was a blissful sound to the men's' ears. Chase drove through the busy streets and then they made the motorway. Chase smiled, changed the gears, and accelerated. The power took the Doctors' breathe away; they merged with the seats as the Ferrari caressed the straight road before them. The music that blared from the radio filled their heads and smiles appeared on their faces, as their fingers slowly released themselves from the sides of the seats that they had clung to through their accelerated fear.

"So, what do you think we should expect?" Murphy asked Chase as they sped past cars.

"He's far more...cool...than we are led to believe. He has an air of ease about everything that he says and does. He's not a lot of trouble, to be honest; I suppose he only kills those who hurt him."

"What about his lawyer?"

"No one knows the truth about anything in his case, really. His lawyer may have defended him but he may not have been a decent guy to him directly, y' know?"

"You were so lucky to get that chance, Chase. It was all due to that girl."

"She wasn't just any girl, she was the reason I got promoted."

"I thought you didn't show Chambers your assignment?" O'Hare asked.

"Are you stupid? Of course I showed him it...just in case an opportunity like this came along, and of course, this baby wouldn't be mine if I didn't earn a little bit extra." He smirked and gripped the leather under his fingers. He turned to the left, heading north. As the engine carried them faster than the other cars that crawled along the motorway, they embraced the pull the car created. Their eyes remained on the road, but their minds were with Norton; they longed to be in his presence and there was an unmistakable excitement in his case. They looked forward to treating a man that had inspired their curiosity and had led them to fill the vacancies for Doctors in a Mental Hospital.

Chapter Twenty-Two

The Nurses and Doctors sat in a circle in the staff room with the door locked.

"There was always a chance this could happen. Shaw will know what to do. Where *is* he? Has anyone been able to contact him or Clarine?" Marie asked. Everyone shook their heads. Marlon stood up.

"It's been three hours since it happened. They'll be awakening now and I think we should follow the plan I put forward earlier."

When no one had any better ideas, they all took a deep breath and stood up; their legs hardly holding their quivering bodies.

Paul and Angelina's bodies had been taken down to the basement, where the morgue was. The morgue had hardly ever been inhabited, and now two members of staff lay dead in its metal mouths and two Officials were missing and couldn't to be found.

The staff walked with vengeance and each step they took was filled with venom and a sore anger. They marched down the steps they had hurled the unconscious bodies down earlier. They had punched and kicked their bodies and had left them black and blue; their flesh torn and cut and their legs, arms, heads and torsos scraped and gashed from the hard stone floor they were drawn over. Their bodies were now in strait jackets—two for each of them. They were chained to the walls where iron hooks protruded from the walls; the rooms obviously used as torture chambers when the hospital had been a Castle.

I awoke to the constricting feel of a strait jacket, and when my eyes looked down, I saw I was wearing two. With a frustrated sigh I realized I had been captured. My thoughts flew to Keelin, and a concerned guilt swept through me. I had subjected her to this world, and goodness knows what they would have done to her; the deceiver and traitor of her colleagues. Then the pain hit me and it seemed it had hit Keelin too; screams and cries soared through the walls and they echoed through the corridor. I could handle *my* pain because I had been subjected to far worse by my parents, so I had never felt much pain when people tried to physically hurt me since then—the one thing I thanked my parents for. Anger welled up in my chest and I felt like screaming to her, but instead I focused on remaining lucid and awaited the entrance of my next victim.

Benjamin and Marlon burst through the door and charged towards me. My head hit the stone wall I was chained to as Marlon's fist hit my face multiple times. I could taste blood in my mouth, and I smiled as my blood seeped through the ridges of my teeth. They took turns to lay their fists into my stomach. I moaned slightly as they kicked my knees. I felt my knee caps shudder as they were weakened. I had had enough. Marlon's face came closer to mine and I could see the lust for vengeance in his eyes.

"You killed my friends so I'm going to kill you," Marlon said through gritted teeth.

"I'd love to see you try," I replied, as a threatening and provocative smirk etched its way onto my face.

"Tell me what you did with Shaw and Clarine," Benjamin said as he stepped closer to me.

"I killed Shaw, and Keelin had the honours of killing Clarine," I said and I stared back into their widening eyes.

"You're a liar. You're just trying to scare us—you don't have the *guts* to kill them," Benjamin said as he slapped my head with the back in his hand.

"They're in the cell beside mine."

I smiled as I saw suspicion mixed with fear fill their eyes. I threw my head forward into Benjamin's as he exchanged a doubtful glance with his colleague. He fell back in surprise. Marlon stood motionless as he watched his friend fall. I head butted him too and he fell back. I felt adrenaline surge through my veins. My adrenaline wasn't normal— mine gave me more strength than most people would ever have imagined.

I focused my power on my arms and as I tensed my muscles I threw them out. The material that constrained me tore from me. I held two pieces of material in my hands and tugged. They tore from the chains and fell against the walls that they had hung tensed from previously. I held the material in my hands and ran towards the two young men scurrying for the door; their shocked bodies proving useless when they wanted to move.

I swung the material across Benjamin's face as I pinned Marlon's neck against the wall by my foot. Benjamin recoiled in pain as the loose buckle of the jacket hit his cheekbone. I swung it again and it hit him on the other side. He fell further to the ground, and then I swung the material into Marlon's face. I threw my fist into Marlon's face as I released my foot. I held both of the men by their necks and lifted them to my full height; their feet dangled and kicked from their airborne position. Their faces pulsated and I threw them against the opposite wall where I had been chained. They fell to the floor in a heap and then they began to scramble over each other as they attempted to stand up.

"You can't kill two men at once," Benjamin said as he clutched his red neck.

"I've done it before and they were the Court Officers—you two will be like a pair of puppies in comparison," I said with a smile. I tasted the blood in my mouth again.

I saw their eyes follow the blood as it trickled from my mouth. I let them fall and I kicked them both in their faces and punched Benjamin until he was unconscious. Then I turned on Marlon as he attempted to claw at the door. I grabbed his collar, threw him on his back and crawled on top of him. I watched him quiver with fear and I heard a squeak of terror extend beyond his lips.

My hands pinched harder as I throttled him. His legs flailed but the power was leaving them rapidly. When he finally ceased to be, I scanned his body for the keys and then stood up, marvelling at my achievement. I walked over to Benjamin and silently killed his breath. The Silence engulfed me like a blanket of glory, and then it was time to help Keelin.

Chapter Twenty-Three

I felt Norton and I become one and I felt his presence within me. In my mind's eye I pictured all that had happened in the Cafeteria. I smiled as I awoke. I was disorientated but as I came to I realized where I was. I was in the dungeons of the Castle, and the basement of the Asylum. I felt restrained and then I realized that I was. I looked down and saw strait jackets hug my torso. I grimaced as I realized the pain my flesh had encountered. I wondered where Norton was. I frowned as I thought of him in the same circumstances as mine.

I heard steps thundering through the corridor and I heard their owners bellow as they approached. I tried to move from my standing position and then I realized I was supported by tense and tight chains that hung from the wall behind me. Nurses and Doctors entered the cell I was contained in, and Fiona Brown emerged from the crowd that had assembled by the door. Fiona produced a small knife and she walked towards me with vengeance smeared across her grimace. She held it out and it was remarkably steady.

"This is for Angelina, my best friend, and Paul." She lunged forward and moved the blade swiftly across my side. I screamed with a pain I had never experienced before. My eyes were wide with the fiery hot pain that surged from the gash as it produced my warm blood. "Tell us where Shaw and Clarine are, and this blade will not taste your blood more than it has to." She stepped back and held it steady in front of my face. I saw my thick blood hang from the sharp blade and I was reduced to tears.

"They're in the cell beside Norton's—they're dead."

"Who killed who?" Fiona asked and the rest of her staff was surprised that *that* was her first question.

"I killed Clarine and Norton killed Shaw." Through tears that hung on the edge of my eye lashes, I saw their faces surge with a feeling of sorrow and I knew my own was bound to increase drastically.

"Why would you kill for him?" Marie asked.

"I love him," I answered. They looked at me with expressions as if I had given them an insufficient answer. "When you love someone, you become a part of them, and I'd kill again, not only for him, but for us."

Fiona had an indifferent expression on her face as she walked towards me again, the knife in her outstretched hand.

"That's not good enough," she said and she slowly cut the flesh on my other side. Then she began jabbing the knife into my legs and arms. I held my breath and wished it to be over. I wanted Norton to save me. I closed my eyes and raised my face to the ceiling. I could feel the blade sear through me. I could feel the blood pour from me, and as I felt it warm my bare feet I called out for him in my mind. I clenched my teeth and as Fiona was dragged away from me, the rest of the Nurses slapped and punched my face. I could feel blood in my mouth and I wanted nothing more than to kill all of them in that instant.

Then their sneering cackles and laughs did cease, as they listened to the noises from their door. I could hear screams echo through the walls and corridor; they were not Norton's screams and I knew he was fighting back. I smiled with relief as they discussed what their next move would be. They decided to leave me there and run for a safe haven, leaving Marlon and Benjamin to their own fate. I smiled and I felt the blood drip from my lips.

"What the hell are you smiling at?" July Hyde said as she slapped me once more, trying to wipe it from my face.

"You criticise us? Look at yourselves, you're just as bad as us," I said with a laugh as I heard the door of the other cell open, and judging by the screams of the people running in the opposite direction, Norton was walking this way. July left me with a lingering stare of hatred before she ran with her crowd down the corridor, away from Norton.

Norton's face, as he turned the corner of the door, was like a wish. I smiled as I saw him. When he stepped further into the light I saw the blood on his face and clothes. I was about to ask what had happened, but I wasn't given the chance. He ran to me and kissed my torn and beaten lips. It was the best feeling I had ever experienced in my life. He wrapped his hands around the chains and tore them from the walls; his strength didn't surprise me because I always knew he had the strength of a wild creature. He held me in his arms as he knelt down. He took the strait jackets off me, now scarlet. His face donned a worried and frantic expression as if he was going to cry. I put my hand on his face and smiled. I kissed him again. I tasted the blood that was on his lips and I knew he had done what I had wanted to do to my oppressors.

"How can I ease the pain?"

"You just did," I said with a smile but he looked at me with concerned and serious eyes. "There is a room down this corridor where we keep extra supplies of pain medication."

He nodded and lifted me in his arms. As he held me gently in his strong arms, I knew I had never felt safer.

I didn't even feel the needle as he pushed it through my skin; the pain previous to that had blocked out any soreness I would feel again. I told him to take some for himself, but he refused.

"Pain is the one thing I wish to embrace while I am still alive and able to feel it. It is the one thing on this earth that reassures existence — that and love." He kissed me and then stared into my eyes. I could see him find himself in them, and his eyes widened. Robert was coming forth completely. I watched, amazed, as his eyes changed; they were changing from green to brown. His eyes brightened and a sensitive man spoke.

"Keelin, you don't know me, but I know you—I love you." Robert kissed me and I could sense a change in his kiss. I looked into his eyes and I saw Rupert lurking in the background; a lovely darkness that filled my mind when I looked deep enough.

"I thought you had become one?"

"We've never experienced some one we love die—it's changed both of us—"

"I don't want one or the other, I want both of you. Can you merge and fully become one man, for me?" He blinked with uncertainty, and then smiled with trust and happiness.

He stood up and took a deep breath and closed his eyes. At that moment a ray of moonlight struck him from a tall and very narrow gap in the wall; the miniature space for air circulation in the dungeons. He held his arms out and it seemed he was floating in the light. The dust motes danced around him and twirled away as he jerked his hands to his head. His hands closed around his head and he laughed with an almost sore but happy pain. Then he relaxed and the moonlight softened as it passed in the sky. He walked over to me and knelt down to me. His eyes were different; one was brown and one was green.

"You did merge," I said after a shocked gasped left my lips.

"I'm one, for you, for us, for the fight for Silence."

"How is it possible?"

He smiled and lifted me in his arms. As he walked out the door, a power in his walk appeared that wasn't there before. I looked up at his face and he smiled. I could see both Rupert and Robert there. He was softer, yet I received the definite sense that he was much stronger and more powerful than his previously lonely and isolated self. I knew I would never understand him completely, but as he held me in his arms, I knew I didn't have to know everything about him; so I smiled and looked into his eyes once more. When I saw a sparkle beyond my reflection in his eyes, I knew if magic dwelled somewhere, it would dwell in those eyes.

Chapter Twenty-Four

They saw Norton's blood stained face approach them from the end of the corridor. Keith Matter remained speechless, simply nudging Thomas Dorian. Thomas and Keith began to back away from him, forgetting to alert the rest to the approaching danger. Justin Breda and Leonard Beau noticed their rapid departure and they began screaming, which created hysteria, and screams of horror escaped and echoed around the walls.

"Is he following us?" Karen Black asked as she followed the corridors through the Asylum. Rebecca looked back and when she saw no one following them, she reassured the group ahead of her. Even with reassurance they didn't stop running until they reached the Cafeteria. In a frenzy and terrified, they shouted in panic for Thomas to open the office door. He fumbled with the keys before they were able to enter.

They forced their way past each other, the motto *each man for himself* obviously key in their minds, as they elbowed each other to get to a safe place quicker. The door was locked when they were all inside and they moved to the back of the office, and submerged themselves in the shadows. The kitchen staff had buried themselves in the corners earlier when the killing had happened, and so their fate was going to be the same as the Nurses' and Doctors'.

Their faces were in the darkness; their bodies motionless and frightened, afraid to move due to the fear that Norton was watching them. Finally, Thomas stood up and took control.

"We have CCTV cameras, we'll keep watching for him and if we see them we'll know where the best place for our attack strategy is, okay?"

They held their quivering bodies and crawled over to the desk where Thomas was standing. Gathering their strength, they pulled up seats and sat in front of the small screens sitting on the desk.

"We have to turn these lights on," Justin said, following Thomas' lead.

"Are you mad? We don't want to tell him we are here," Joy Fay said. Justin nodded in defeat. They sat and watched the screens as the darkness enveloped them further.

When their eyes had begun to deceive them and they had thought they had seen Norton in the shadows of many floors, they actually saw him. He was walking down the first floor corridor with Keelin in his arms. Their eyes grew wide as he began to turn for the Cafeteria. If they had been any less scared, screams would have left them, but the fear they were experiencing was paralyzing. Their eyes all left the screen and moved their way across the office glass to where the doors were. In the darkness was a figure of a man standing still and looking at them.

Norton smiled as the Silence met him. He looked up at the shadowed faces in the office. He mouthed *I'll be back* and he walked off. They all knew exactly what he had said, and their eyes immediately focused back on the screen they had seen him on. They all watched Norton walk through the corridor, illuminated only by the dim lights that hung from the ceiling.

Norton was moving up the stairs to the second floor where the patients were. They remained motionless, their eyes following the killer as he moved his way around the Asylum.

Chapter Twenty-Five

I knew I would be saved by her. I loved her so much. I knew her words would heal my tortured mind and that my trust and love in her would help me.

I stood up in the basement, Rupert smiled in my mind, and he told me he wanted this too. I beckoned the moon in my one wish; *make my final hours with her beautiful and perfect. Please unite us and please take us away from this place in perfect solace, silence, love and beauty.* I could feel the moonlight soar through the darkness and hit my mind and heart with a magical beauty that made wishes real and true. I could feel Rupert merge with me, and I felt me merge with him. We were becoming one. I could feel the power of both our minds, bodies and souls unite and form a strength that would conquer all; the strength created by love. I opened my eyes and I knew we were new.

I am a new person. I had changed through love; that's *always* a good way to change.

I carried her in my arms up the stairs that led to the second floor, where the patients were. I was going to silence them, and then go back to the Cafeteria to kill the rest. My heart beat faster as I felt the tortured minds yonder. I could definitely sense I was some-one different— I wasn't going to silence them, they didn't need silencing, because the Silence had rescued them from a harsh world a long time ago. Now I was going to free them from this cage that they had spent so many years in. They would feel Nature once more in their lives beyond these walls. I took a deep breath and sat Keelin on the floor by the stairs; the moonlight bouncing off her flowing hair, and the light the moon reflected in her eyes as they smiled at me.

Chapter Twenty-Six

Silent men sat upright in their beds as they heard Norton approach. Their logical minds told them to be very afraid, because their death was near, but their hearts, their deeper minds and their most loyal friend, Silence, told them not to fear, because he was here to save them from a prolonged peril, and reunite them with the Nature their hearts and minds had longed to embrace for so long.

Kevin sat on the edge of his bed and heard the slow, steady and free foot-steps as they felt the coldness of the stone as they stopped beyond his door. Kevin took one last look at the moon through his window and awaited the fate he had been told to trust. Norton's hand wrapped around the door handle and turned the skeleton key in the door. The face that greeted him was different; it was softer, calmer and more smiling.

A smiling face met Kevin's and he stood up and put out his hand for Norton to shake. Norton grasped it and pulled Kevin into a tight hug. Kevin felt relief that he hadn't felt in so long: he felt free. A tear etched its way along his dusty and forgotten face. Kevin's mind honoured Norton and spoke words from his heart: *My saviour*. Norton smiled and brought Kevin back into the corridor. Kevin looked around the corridor he had seen for so many years, but now it seemed more alive than ever. He walked with Norton as they freed the rest of the forgotten men. Kevin took off his shoes and followed Norton's suit. His feet breathed for what seemed the first time as they met the cold stone beneath them.

Man after man followed him as Norton freed them, bringing them to Nature, where she simply loves them and lets them be. When every man on the second floor had been saved, he walked back to Keelin who was waiting with a smile for him. As the distance closed, Norton ran to her. Her smiles were becoming weak. Norton kissed her and she smiled with more life, as if his love was energy in itself; it was definitely something to stay alive for.

"I will shelter you from all of the pain," Norton said as he kissed her again, and lifted her in his arms. He walked up to the third floor and gave the key to Kevin. "Liberate your fellow men," Norton said. Kevin smiled with a gratitude that was beyond words. Norton focused on the woman in his arms. He knew she would only have a few hours left. He was filled with a longing in his chest he had never felt before; he didn't want her to go. He could have held her forever, and he knew he would, in another time and space, where they could simply be.

Kevin arrived back to Norton's presence with his army of free men behind him. He smiled down at them from his height, and he knew the time had come to silence the evil creatures who cowered in the Cafeteria, almost awaiting his presence. He kissed Keelin once more and put her in Kevin's arms. Kevin looked confused yet honoured.

"Guard her with your life. Meet me by the Cafeteria in half an hour. I'm going to silence our tormenters."

Kevin nodded, and as Norton turned to walk away he felt a delicate hand on his. Keelin brought him closer to him. She kissed him for luck, and he felt like he had all the luck in the world on his lips at that very moment.

Chapter Twenty-Seven

Meanwhile, Chase, Murphy and O'Hare sped towards the coast, where the Asylum was situated. The moon's light fell heavily on the black surface of the Ferrari. Their tired eyes blinked heavily but they were nearly there. Chase accelerated again as he drove down another road to his right, leading them closer to their destination.

"We should be there in the next hour or so lads, just hang in there," he told the men, whose heads were drooping due to the sleep that attempted to engulf them. Chase turned on the radio again and they repositioned in their seats. "Come on, lads, you're in a *Ferrari*, enjoy the experience, because I'm sure these journeys will be the only time your lucky asses ever find a seat in one." He threw a bottle of water at Murphy and told him to drink it, and then he did the same to O'Hare. The water sat on Murphy's lips and then his eyes closed again. O'Hare tensed his hand and slapped Murphy's cheek.

"What the hell?" Murphy said. Chase cackled from his seat. Murphy repositioned himself in the seat and caressed his neck, which was sore from the awkward position he had fallen asleep in. "I'm up!" Murphy screamed as O'Hare's hand attempted to smack him again. O'Hare laughed from the back seat.

"I'm *hungry*," O'Hare said. Chase turned the radio down and looked in his rear mirror as he spoke to O'Hare.

"Did we or did we not stop for food a few hours ago? We'll get food when we get there. I *promise* you your appetite will vanish when you see Norton." Chase nodded as O'Hare's eyes lit up. "As I said, we'll be there in an hour or so, so just relax and enjoy the rest of the ride." He accelerated again, and the two men sat up, enjoying the pull the car had when it went as it went faster.

Chapter Twenty-Eight

The staff had stared at the screens in shock as they showed Norton liberating the men and then one particular patient liberating the rest under Norton's command.

"He's gathering an army to kill us," Leonard said.

"No. He's coming to fight us himself," Thomas said. They watched his figure as it ran down the stairs and through the corridors.

"The police will be here soon, anyway, all we have to do is fight him off."

"The police are coming?"

"Well, I presume *someone* called them when he killed Paul and Angelina?"

Silence answered Justin's question.

"Did *no one* phone the police?" Keith said in a frightened voice.

"Either every one of you is as *stupid* as hell, or did you all think we *didn't need* them?" Justin asked, stamping his foot in fury.

"Oh shut up. *You* could have phoned them too," Karen said.

"We were all so shocked we forgot about calling for help," Joy said in a hoarse voice.

"This is just *great*," Thomas said and he threw the chair away from under him.

"We're all going to *die*," Marie said. She looked at her blood stained hands. "He's going to come for me first—I sliced Keelin." She began quivering. "Do something. *Help me*," she said as she clung to Thomas, her panic stricken face in his. He pushed her away from him and walked to the glass that looked out onto the Cafeteria.

"We're just going to have to fight him. We'll beat him, I promise you all," Thomas said and as he turned around and met faces of fright and terror. He looked around just in time to see Norton run towards the glass. His eyes met his and then they were splintered with glass as Norton smashed his way through.

His hands found Thomas' neck and jerked it. He went limp and lifelessly fell onto the desk beside him. He looked at the scared faces of the people in front of him. Norton defended himself as chairs hurtled in his direction. He saw people run for the door but he was too fast for them. He darted through the darkness and barred the door with his large body. They recoiled in fear.

I grabbed the Nurse who was in front of me and throttled her. My strength increased and I hardly realized I had broken her neck in my grip. I frowned as I looked at my hands but then I smiled. On my command the staff moved out of the office, but they were all bearing syringes like swords, moving in a group like frightened animals. They edged towards me with their sedative armour. I laughed as I looked at their weapons.

"Let us go and we'll not say this to anyone," Justin said. His syringe was aimed at my face. I grabbed it before he had even realized; it seemed my reflexes and instincts were sharper and faster too. I crushed it in my hand, and their eyes watched the sedative as it poured over my fingers and dripped onto the floor. Deciding all else was lost, they all began to run at me with their full force.

After throwing them far from me, I ran from one to the other and silenced one at a time. Some jumped from table to table in some way of keeping out of danger, but that simply made it more of a game for me. I had more strength than I had ever had, and I *loved* it. There was only one Nurse left when my killing spree was done.

"It's funny, I was nearly certain you were going to kill me first," Marie said.

"I'm unpredictable, you should know that by now," I said and I ran after her as she sped around the Cafeteria. When I caught up with her she turned suddenly and stopped. I ran into her and we fell over. She cackled loudly as she let go of the knife that was in my chest. I could feel my heart pulse against the metal as it sat in between my ribs. I looked at her, my breathing sharp and shallow, each breath sharp and painful. She tried to free herself, but I grabbed her and put my hands on her throat. I began to crush her veins and then I heard words spill from her discoloured lips.

"It's ironic—that's the knife I used to slice your girlfriend. I'm killing both of you." She tried to laugh but she couldn't. Tears welled up in my eyes and then I crushed her neck. The Silence that remained after was blissful. I knew only one thing that had to be done now; I had to die with Keelin.

Chapter Twenty-Nine

Chase drove along the forest path that led to the Asylum. They were half an hour from meeting Norton and as their eyes scoured the forest shadows crept on them. Chase stopped the car and they sat silently in the car. Chase locked the doors from the button by him.

"I've got this strong feeling that something is dreadfully wrong," Chase said as his sweaty hands gripped the steering wheel that he sat motionless behind.

"I feel that, too, Chase. Do you think we should call Chambers?" Murphy said as beads of sweat began to form on his skin.

"That is the *last* thing we do," Chase said.

"We should carry on and find the place, and then decide what we feel when we get there. I mean, there *is* something dreadfully wrong; we're visiting a schizophrenic serial killer—we should be keeping well away from him. If there was something really wrong we would have been informed by now," O'Hare said.

"Okay. You're right. This is just a precaution, alright?" Chase said and he opened the glove compartment—a gun greeted them. He took it out and put it in Murphy's lap. Murphy held his hands up as if Chase was pointing it at him. "Just keep it in your lap, and if something or someone attacks us, use it, okay?" Murphy did not answer but remained focused on the gun in his lap. Chase felt more at ease, knowing he was armed, and began driving through the forest again; it was clear by the overgrowth that hardly anyone had travelled through here by car in a very long time. The moon shone against the tall trees and made their shadows look like soldiers defending their fortress that lay beyond this forest by the sea.

Chapter Thirty

I stumbled out of the Cafeteria, my hand exerting pressure on the wound at my heart. I had pulled the dagger out of my chest and had put it in my pocket. I looked down the corridor and saw fifty men walk through the corridor. Kevin was leading them and he was carrying a beautiful woman in his arms. I ran to him, and he halted aghast as his eyes looked at my chest that was rapidly pouring my blood. I put my arms under her and Kevin nervously handed her to me. I held Keelin in my arms. Her eyes opened and she smiled weakly. I kissed her and energy filled me too. I looked at Kevin and the rest of the men awaiting instruction.

"You must cleanse the dead with the moonlit sea. Take the dead from this place and give them to the sea—the moon shall sail them to their rightful place." Kevin held out the skeleton key in his palm and nodded. "After that, run into the forest and live—simply be, live with Nature, and live the rest of your lives as free and liberated men." I smiled as their eyes widened at the thought. Smiles, cheers and laughs erupted and I nodded at them respectfully and with gratitude. "My death is coming, men, and I'm thankful, because I am with her as death also finds her." I turned and stepped slowly towards the door that led outside. I felt her hand on my face and I looked into her eyes. We were both moving toward death in Silence, but I was so joyous that I could happily die with her. I continued walking until we reached the door. I put my back to the door and pushed.

The cold breeze meandered around us as my toes moved through the soft grass that grew on the grounds. I hadn't felt the earth against my skin in so long. I absorbed the freshness of the world as it welcomed us. We came to the fence that separated the wilderness from us. I lay Keelin on the soft grass, and then I ran against it. The wood splintered and flew away. There was a gap in the fence now, and I lifted Keelin into my arms again and carried her through it.

The wood that welcomed us was beautiful. I looked down and saw Keelin's eyes brighten as the ultimate beauty of Nature met her. She ran her hands against the trees as we walked by them; her hands feeling the rough bark that contained an old magic, and ultimately, the treasures of the Earth. The moon shone brighter than I had ever seen it. I thought perhaps it was because it was about to carry us through time that it appeared brighter, but it didn't matter to me; my whole world was in my vision. I had never felt happier. The slope made the dirt follow my feet as they stepped over it. I felt Nature wrap itself around me, and I never wanted this to end, but I knew a better and happier place awaited Keelin and me.

The swell of the sea met our eyes and ears suddenly as we moved out of the dense forest. I had never seen the sea more beautiful; the moon delicately danced and shimmered on the waves as they moved with strength and power. Keelin kissed me and we sat by a willow tree as it bent to the water. I could feel my heart pump the last of the blood from my body. Keelin looked at my chest—she hadn't realized I had been hurt. She looked scared and worried and then I pulled out the knife that I had placed in my pocket. Tears cleansed her blood stained skin as she took hold of the knife.

"The same thing is killing us," she whispered. I smiled and kissed her forehead as she nestled close to my body.

"The same thing is also saving us."

We looked out at the sea, and we listened to the gentle sway of the ocean as it met the shore. My back felt the soft willow and Keelin felt it too. I smiled as she kissed my hands. Our fingers ran over one another's. We listened to the sound of the world—gentle, free and happy.

"We fought for Silence, Keelin, and we won," I said.

"Is this what true Silence sounds like?" Keelin asked as her eyes followed the waves as they moved the willow gently.

"It sounds like *this*—when the noises of an ignorant world cease to be, it is in Nature that true Silence is found—it's the sound of happiness." I smiled as tears left my eyes. I knew my time was approaching. I was so happy that the silence of the world was with me. She coughed slightly and I knew her time was approaching too.

"I want to hear this forever." Keelin whispered.

"You will." We looked at each other and we kissed. In that kiss I saw all the things we had done, seen and said when we were together. She held me tighter and I held her closer still.

"Thank you for loving me, saving me and finding me," I said as I saw the moonlight reach us.

"I want to remain in your arms forever," she said.

"I'll hold you forever." I could see in her eyes a scared anticipation. "Don't be afraid, Keelin, I'm with you, and you'll never be alone." She smiled and I saw the moonlight find her eyes. She rested her head on my chest, and I heard her last breaths escape her. Her fingers clung to mine and as the moonlight found her completely.

"I love you..."

The moonlight crossed her body and found my eyes. I looked into the sky and I could see Silence find me. Through a striking beauty I saw Keelin's face. I clung to her body. I took my last breath and fell into an abyss of happiness—greater than any I had ever encountered. I was truly happy, with Keelin in my arms forever.

"I'll love you forever..."

Chapter Thirty-One

The wheels of the Ferrari crushed the twigs as they rolled slowly over them as the car neared the grounds of the Asylum. The Asylum was surrounded by the dense forest they had just driven through, and it certainly was the creepiest place they had ever seen in their lives.

"You were here before, Chase, what are you so scared about?" Murphy asked. Chase was quivering in his seat.

"That was in the daytime. This is different. Look, we'll park at the front and ring them." He directed the car through the gates that automatically opened for cars to enter, but not to leave, Chase thought. He turned off the engine as he stopped at the open front doors. The lights in the car went out as he turned off the engine. The men suddenly became very nervous. The darkness surrounded them and their eyes began to fool them. ""I think I'll keep the engine running." Chase said. He turned the key. The lights illuminated three men standing in front of the car. The three men in the car screamed louder than they had ever screamed in their lives. The three men in black trousers and white shirts darted off out of the light and ran for the forest. There was a splintering off wood heard as they charged through the wooden fence and escaped into the woods.

"WHO THE HELL WAS THAT?" Chase screamed as he hit all around him in what could only be perceived as a frantic panic mixed with a dreadful fear. Murphy was holding the gun in front of him, aiming it at where the men had stood. O'Hare's eyes had followed them as they had barged through the fence.

"Were those men patients?" O'Hare gasped.

"If they were the patients where is the staff?"

"What the hell is that?" Chase pointed at the far end of the grounds. He put his full beams on and in the light they saw a man in black and white trousers carrying a man over his shoulder into the forest through a gap in the fence. Their mouths fell open as they realized it was a Doctor.

"Reverse and get out of here now!" Murphy shouted, aiming the gun at Chase. Chase grabbed the gun and held it in his hand.

"You don't even know how to hold that properly, never mind shoot it! I don't think those automatic gates work from the inside. I'll ring the office." He took out his phone and dialled the number Chambers had given them for this Asylum's Head Office. Chase tried three times before concluding that no one was going to answer it. "We're going to have to go into those woods." He said. He received only angry faces.

"Sorry, but did you see what just happened?" Murphy said sarcastically.

"Look, that can't be the only Doctor, and they seem to be running for the woods anyway. There could be people hurt and in danger down there, and we have no way out anyway." He turned off the engine and looked at how many bullets he had in the gun.

"What are you turning the car off for? If we're going out there, we're going through that forest in *your* car...*you're* the one who wants to go down there." O'Hare said as he leant forward. Chase turned around to O'Hare and began slapping his head.

"Don't be so *stupid*!" Chase said to O'Hare's comment. "Get out, we're going now!"

"*We* don't have weapons!" Murphy said, pointing to the gun.

"Well, I'm afraid I don't have all my ammo with me tonight!" He said sarcastically. When he received only stubborn faces, he said, "Okay, there's a baseball bat in the boot and I think there's a few golf clubs."

He got out of the car and edged nervously to the back of the car, staying very close to the car. He opened the boot and took out what he had described. O'Hare and Murphy took deep breaths and then followed Chase. They felt braver with weapons in their grasp, and they looked around for any psychopaths that were running loose. Chase closed the boot.

Three strong Doctors began walking towards the gap in the fence. As they walked, their egos began to mount and with each step they took they changed from Doctors into warriors. Chase was in the middle with a gun in one hand and a golf club in the other. Murphy walked to the right of him with a baseball bat in his hand. O'Hare walked to the left of Chase with two golf clubs in either hand. They looked like they were ready to fight, but they secretly hoped they wouldn't have to.

Their eyes became accustomed to the darkness, and their vision turned from colour to black and white. Chase stepped through the gap first, and then the other two followed him. It was the eeriest place they had ever witnessed. They had seen scenes like this in horror films, and they hated the way the characters they were now representing usually turned out.

They gripped their weapons as they walked down the slope, dodging from tree to tree, keeping alert if they heard something. They could smell the sea and they knew the end of their descent was near. A deafening silence engulfed them, and they nearly dropped their weapons when they saw the sight that befell them. Their eyes fell on the sea where twenty or so bodies ebbed and flowed with the waves. They couldn't see any survivors as they ran to the shore and looked closer at the awful scene.

"Have you still got that appetite?" Chase asked O'Hare. They didn't know whether it was a nervous reaction or whether they were going crazy themselves, but they all began to laugh. Their laughing only stopped when Chase saw two shadows by the Willow tree.

Keelin and Norton were approached quietly by the three men. Their faces grew paler than the moon and their weapons really did fall to the floor in shock. Chase knelt down and put his fingers to both their necks. All the fear and anxiety left them as they looked at the two dead lovers, cradling one another, the moonlight shining through the swaying willow, decorating their bodies with an array of moonlit magic.

"Who is she?" Murphy asked, looking at Chase's sombre face.

"That's Keelin Hogan...and Norton." Chase answered, a silent respect flowing from him.

"Oh....my...God..." That was the only sound that appeared in the silent scene after that. They stood by the sea, looking at the two lovers who lay dead in each other's arms, with the rays of moonlight highlighting the magic, the silence and the beauty of their love.

www.ingramcontent.com/pod-product-compliance
Lightning Source LLC
Chambersburg PA
CBHW030134260626
47156CB00008B/2934